Conversation With My Mother
Novel

Wonder Guchu

Mwanaka Media and Publishing Pvt Ltd,
Chitungwiza Zimbabwe
*
Creativity, Wisdom and Beauty

Publisher: *Mmap*
Mwanaka Media and Publishing Pvt Ltd
24 Svosve Road, Zengeza 1
Chitungwiza Zimbabwe
mwanaka@yahoo.com
mwanaka13@gmail.com
www.africanbookscollective.com/publishers/mwanaka-media-and-publishing
https://facebook.com/MwanakaMediaAndPublishing/

Distributed in and outside N. America by African Books Collective
orders@africanbookscollective.com
www.africanbookscollective.com

ISBN: 978-1-77934-541-7
EAN: 9781779345417

© Wonder Guchu 2025

DISCLAIMER
All views expressed in this publication are those of the author and do
not necessarily reflect the views of *Mmap*.

*M*ama, I have returned home. I have come back to where my umbilical cord is buried.

You always told me I was born on the way to the clinic, by the giant fig tree that is now just a stump.

That stump has been licked by veldt fires, lit by small boys hunting for mice. You never stopped reminding me that you delivered me alone in the veldt.

You told me that while you lay on the bare ground, regaining your strength, the ants of the veldt licked my skin, searching for the softest spot to break in.

In your weak state, you tried hard to keep them away. I often feel that even today there are ants looking for soft spots in my life to break in.

I have come back, *Mama*, to bury myself where my siblings lie cold and dead. I tried, *Mama*, to run away as far as I could from returning to my undug hungry grave. That place is reserved for me in the foothills of Nyota Mountain.

It is always the place we all end up—our destination. We travel the world, but all the roads we take lead us nowhere but to the foothills of Nyota Mountain.

And this mountain, *Mama*, has been waiting. It is waiting now. Motionless and emotionless. Every time we bury people in the foothills, I visualise Nyota Mountain opening up her arms and then closing them after we pile earth on top of the graves.

I am back, *Mama*. I am back to bury myself. I am not afraid of dying, Mama, but what scares me is the thought of people walking away after covering my grave.

I always have this image of those church women singing those sad songs while the men shovel earth and pile up stones on my grave.

I just wish that Kamukwasha's wife will not be the one singing at my graveside. Her voice closes doors and gives so much hopelessness. I want *Mai* Joyce to sing for me when my coffin is being lowered into the ground. *Mai* Joyce has a sweet voice that makes it easier and more comfortable for anyone to sleep forever.

I have listened to her singing at most burials, and she makes it impossible to imagine that there could be a resurrection one day.

The gravediggers, *Mama*, they joke about the dead. They joke about their lives and a lot of other things that I cannot talk to you about.

Do you still remember Jarata, *Mama*? That tall, lanky man who could dig a grave alone? Jarata did it with so much ease, Mama. I saw him digging graves while the rest of the men sat and joked.

I am not afraid of death, *Mama*. How can I be when you have all gone before me? But this vivid image of women walking ahead in single file with men following them after a burial makes me shiver. They walk always each with their hands folded behind and humming under their breath.

It makes me wonder how it feels to be alone for the first time in the womb of the earth on the first day.

And when night falls and the foothills grow dark, and the insects make all sorts of sounds, those owls that hoot and flap their wings in the night, *Mama*, where do they come from?

And the jackals too, *Mama*, do you remember how they howl whenever we bury someone?

It is as if they are welcoming the newly departed. Will I hear the cicadas and crickets filling the night with their songs, *Mama*?

I see my grave as the only fresh one among the old graves, and I will be the latest one lying under there, being welcomed by all those creatures of the night.

It gets eerily quiet in the foothills of Nyota Mountain, *Mama*. The darkness there swirls and sometimes shifts as passing vehicle lights push the shadows farther into the mountain.

I am not afraid of dying, *Mama*, but the first night alone and the thought that I will be there until maybe judgment day, if there ever will be one, scares me.

Yes, *Mama*, death does not scare me, but the rains do. It rained the day we buried Baba. It poured all night long. There was lightning and thunder too.

Sekuru Taurai said rains after a burial were a good sign. He said the departed would have welcomed the newly departed. He said the skies would be crying too, but this time tears of joy.

Do you think, *Mama*, that *Sekuru* Taurai was telling the truth? If he was telling the truth, and if *Baba* was indeed welcomed, why was his grave damaged by the heavy rains?

The rains washed away the earth from *Baba*'s grave. The rain dug into the edges of the grave. There was water standing in puddles on the grave.

I am afraid, *Mama*, that the rain will seep into my grave and damage my coffin. I would love to lie in a dry, warm place without the discomfort of water dripping in through the roof of the grave.

I have come, *Mama*. I have come to bury myself.

Coming back almost three decades later, *Mama*, it feels like I'm arriving in a different place. So much has changed here. This bus stop didn't exist when I left.

There used to be a large muhacha tree there, but now only the burnt stump remains. People used to sit on rocks, waiting for the only bus we called Chemakura, as it traveled along the road through the fields.

This road was a dry path that went through the fields and went around Nyota's head, which blocked its way. I remember a fight between the men from our village, led by *Babamunini* Patrick, and some men from Gomwe in the Kanhukamwe area.

Babamunini Patrick was a small man who threw strong and fast punches that often resulted in split lips and bleeding noses. I remember gathering that Sunday before Chemakura arrived to watch the men fight.

It was a chaotic scene that ended when one of the men pulled out a long knife, causing the men from our village to scatter into Nyota Hills.

Now, this new road is a wide, paved highway that has eroded a large part of the mountain's landscape, only to reemerge on the other side.

This is the same Nyota where we grazed cattle, chased away baboons and monkeys, picked *mazhanje* (loquat-like fruits), and hunted rabbits.

When we were growing up here, you remember *Mama*, the elders used to tell stories about a long serpent that lived in the caves up in Nyota. They said that the snake slithered along tree tops.

Whenever the elders wanted to scare us, they would talk about that snake. It was called *rovambira*. The snake got its name from how it hunted rabbits by striking them on the head.

Only one person claimed to have seen that snake. Nicholas told us one day that he came across the *rovambira* while stealing *mbanje* (marijuana) that unknown people were growing in the hills. *Rovambira*, or any snake for that matter, we were told, had a liking for *mbanje*.

Nicholas said that while he was busy harvesting the drug, he saw the bloodshot eyes of the *rovambira*, which had its head raised high, ready to strike him on the head. But he quickly composed himself and ran away.

The snake chased him, and Nicholas ran and zigzagged through the trees as the snake slithered from one tree to another.

It was crashing through branches and hissing like a storm - Nicholas dramatically told us.

Nicholas, a small man with discoloured lips from smoking, managed to outrun the snake and lived to tell the tale.

I heard that he has since died. His lifeless body was found in his small hut on the outskirts of his mother's homestead near Nyota's head. He never got married or had children.

When I was growing up here, you remember *Mama*, Nyota was always green. Trees covered the rocks and from a distance, the trees gave Nyota a beautiful green layer. Today, Nyota has been stripped bare. I wonder, too, if the *rovambira* still lives there. That is, if there ever was any such snake. Nyota's apex, where the Johanne Masowe sect had a shrine, is barren.

Do you remember, *Mama*, how the sect members would wake the village up early every Friday when they sang like angels. The caves echoed their voices and sent them to the villages below. Sometimes, the sect members would line up across the bare rocky area facing the east. They would be dressed in white flowing robes and moving as one white cloud.

I remember that at one time, the leader of the sect – *Madzibaba* Phillip was his name - once tried to fly from the top of that jutting rock that sat on top of Nyota's hump.

Madzibaba Phillip asked his people to sing for him every Friday to prepare him for the flight to Heaven. While they sang and danced, *Madzibaba* Phillip would be standing barefoot on the rock, arms widespread and eyes shut.

There was a countdown to the day when he would finally take off. Before that day, the sect members gathered at the shrine for a week, singing and fasting.

The village had never been interested in what was happening in the hills especially involving the apostolic sect. But this flight to heaven attracted the attention of our community and those beyond.

Word spread fast that *Madzibaba* Phillip would fly to Heaven just like the Biblical Elijah did. *Madzibaba* Phillip would take off while his congregation and some villagers watched, unlike Elijah who was snatched away by a chariot of fire and horses before Elisha's eyes.

When the day for take-off came, the mountain was dead quiet after a night of song and praise. We also woke up very early not to miss this spectacle. That morning, fog blanketed Nyota as if to help *Madzibaba* Phillip fly to heaven.

The mist drifted from the top to the village and then swirled back to the mountain as if an invisible hand was turning it over. Before the fog disappeared, it sat on top of Nyota Hills and then, like a cloth, started to tear away from the hem.

When the fog disappeared, we saw *Madzibaba* Phillip standing still on top of the hill. He wore white garments. His arms were spread wide. For a long moment, he stood there, and we held our breath. Then the singing started. It was a slow and low rhythm that picked up a crescendo. The mountain echoed the songs and sent them floating down to the villages below.

We all stood outside, watching in marvel at what was about to happen. The singing went on for about an hour, and each time it picked a crescendo. Then without warning, *Madzibaba* Phillip leapt, floated briefly in the air, and came crashing down into the trees.

One of his white garments came loose when he was going down. It drifted in the wind and then disappeared when *Madzibaba* Phillip went down into the trees.

We did not see *Madzibaba* Phillip for months, and his followers said, without shame, he had flown to Heaven. They said the angels had snatched him while he was crashing and took him away.

The followers repeated this until it almost became real until one day, when we were herding cattle in the hills, we saw smoke coming from a cave.

When we checked, we saw *Madzibaba* Phillip lying on a white cloth and being nursed by a group of women.

As I stand here, *Mama*, I feel like a stranger. The spirit that used to walk this land is dead. It is gone. Maybe gone too are those fat rabbits that used to sunbathe every morning. And those monkeys that made love while running and the baboons that fought for love.

That male baboon – the *horomba* we called *Chiwororo* – loved women from the village. It was as big as a lion. It never ran away from us when it came down the hills. With its bloodied buttocks, the baboon would saunter along, turning its head to check.

It constantly barked and grunted and grumbled. It moved alone and invaded maize fields alone. It was a stealthy operator, and most people would only realise that it had been in the field after it had left.

The women were scared of *Chivororo* because he would sit on top of a tree, watching them bathing in the gardens close to the hills. This is why there was talk about *Chivororo* having a soft spot for the village women.

I wonder as I stand here, *Mama*, long after the bus has gone, if there are still baboons of *Chivororo's* calibre in the Nyota Hills after it has been stripped bare.

The rocks are like the bones of a sick person, *Mama*.

Jutted.

Exposed.

Dusty.

Burnt.

Browned.

If it were 30 years ago, the bus would have left a trail of dust, but now the road is tarred and straight like a swollen finger.

From here where I stand, I can see the road narrowing as it disappears into the distance where Rosa Township is or was because I am not sure whether what I knew then is still there. Some mirages rise and tremble with the wind. It is as if there is a fire burning.

Once when we were young, we ran towards the mirages, thinking it was a stream of water flowing across the road. But the mirages kept on shifting until they disappeared into the distance.

The bus I have just alighted from has gone that way. It is not in any way like Chemakura that used to rumble and grumble as it ascended the steep slope at *Mbuya* Nahanda's bus stop.

You still remember *Mbuya* Nehanda, *Mama*? She claimed to be possessed by the spirit of *Mbuya* Nehanda, the great spirit medium killed in 1898 and hanged on the tree near State House in Harare. I know you may not know about State House but we used to talk about *Mbuya* Nehanda helping the *vakomana* during the war.

Do you remember how we were told that *Mbuya* Nehanda's spirit would protect the *vakomana*? That before she was hanged, she prophesied about the war – Chimurenga two – saying her bones will rise and fight back? So, the *vakomana* were her bones that rose and carried out arms to take back the country from the colonists.

This *Mbuya* Nehanda who lived close our village was one of so many other scattered around the country who claimed to be possessed by the spirit of the great spirit medium.

The bus I have come with is a sleek vehicle that glides with the swiftness of the wind. Unlike Chemakura that was dusty inside and would sometimes have some of its windows broken; leaving the passengers to swallow wind and dust, this one has clean seats and a carpet that swallows passengers' feet.

Riding Chemakura was like walking in a sand storm because one would arrive covered in dust that left only eyes and lips visible.

But we loved Chemakura - the young and the old. Chemakura was a marvel to watch. That was why we all would run to the road to watch and wave as Chemakura rolled past, swirling up dust and leaving a trail of black smoke that would hang around the air for hours.

We never got tired of watching and waving at Chemakura, even on the days when it would have brought nobody from the city.

There were days when the villagers would just wait by the big *muchakata* tree anticipating that Chemakura would bring someone they knew from the city.

We would be there – men and women and children. We would be there talking and laughing and waiting.

And when Chemakura never brought anyone from the village, the driver would slow down and wave at the crowd.

His name was Muza. We just knew him as Muza. We never got to know what his second or first name was. He was just Muza. Most bus drivers are known by just one name.

Every morning, villagers would hear Chemakura struggling to climb the rise at Jega, where there used to be a big shop that sold everything. The building has always been there. It belonged to a white man who left it and was then taken over by a businessman who also abandoned it and was taken up by another.

I am unsure how many people tried to run the big shop and failed. In the end, the store stood there – white in the sun, deserted and dying with time.

From here, mama, I can see the shop's roof. I am sure another businessman was trying to revive the big store that seems too big to manage.

Every day, we heard Chemakura sigh as it got to the top of the rise. Then the engine would calm down as the bus descended into Ruya River Bridge before it stopped at Muroyiwa bus stop and then Rosa Township.

Usually, people from this village would start to prepare to catch the bus when they heard it negotiating the steep slopes at Shopo or Shutu villages.

Of course, Chemakura had space for everybody. It was never full. There would be people standing. There would be people sitting. There would be people sitting on other people's laps. There would be children crying because of heat. There would be luggage everywhere, leaving no room for standing. There would be boxes full of tomatoes, sweet potatoes, or even vegetables.

There would be dust everywhere - on the seats, the windows, the floors, and passengers' faces. There would be life as villagers greet each other and ask about life, families, and harvests. They also talked about death and sickness.

On top of the bus would be more boxes and sacks full of green products for sale in Glendale or Mbare Musika in the city.

There were times when there would be goats tied onto the roof. The goats would have their bodies in sacks except for their heads.

The conductor would then leap from one headrest to the next on his way from the door to the back of the bus. He would give out tickets and receive money.

He would leap from one seat to the next and scribble destinations and departure points in a handwriting he alone understood and could read. The only legible on the tickets were the amounts paid.

Chemakura carried everything. Chemakura never left anyone behind. And we loved Chemakura. This was why we never failed to cheer the bus every day when it rolled past this village.

Do you remember my sister Manekaidzo, *Mama*? You brought her on the earth sad. My sister Manekaidzo was born a tiny baby with big sad eyes that blinked after a long time. I was just seven or so at the time of Manekaidzo's birth. I recall how you spent nights awake trying to calm Manekaidzo.

She survived eight miserable months. She died a sad death one night. Her small coffin made of planks from an old wooden grain storage door looked sad too. We were all sad when she died.

She also refused to suckle, and from an early age, you would force her to eat soft porridge. But every time she ate, she vomited.

Her birth that was supposed to be a joy for us all, turned into despair. Manekaidzo never grew or gained weight. Instead, she shrank each day right before our eyes. Her situation took a heavy toll not only on you, mama, but father too.

In the end, about eight or so months after her birth, Manekaidzo had to spend all the time sleeping. Never eating. Never opening her big sad eyes for long. And if she opened them, she would never look at anyone.

We wake up one day to hear you screaming. You had Manekaidzo in your arms. We gathered around you, looking at the limp body and the sad eyes that were not blinking anymore.

When she died, Manekaidzo had been reduced to a small bundle of sadness. There was sadness in her eyes all the time. There was sadness in the way her small, emaciated body drooped. There was sadness. Just sadness. A lot of sadness.

And I stayed sad for some time whenever I passed by her small, sad grave marked out by a small heap of sad stones on the banks of Munwahuku.

I hear, *Mama*, that the valley where we buried Manekaidzo has now been turned inside out by gold panners. I hear the gold panners have also turned the whole grazing area inside out. I also hear that they have dug up Munwahuku's riverbank, where the children's graves used to be.

I always wonder, mama, why would someone like Manekaidzo endure so much sadness.

We usually took our cattle to graze along Munwahuku's banks. There were gardens there too—gardens where sugar cane grew tall and thick. When the war came, some *vakomana* would hide in the sugar cane all day long.

I never told you this *Mama*, but our first encounter with *vakomana* was in *ambuya va*Kachana's garden where we stole sugar cane.

The soldiers had closed schools then, and we spent much of our time herding cattle or just loitering around the protected village.

Those keep or protected villages constructed by Ian Smith's government in 1974. There were 21 such keeps here in Chiweshe.

Every village was deserted from Gweshe to Bare when people were transported into the keeps guarded by district assistants. We called them DAs. There were two gates to every keep. A high fence surrounded the keep itself with barbed wire at the top.

Lorries driven by soldiers came to transport people from this village sometime in 1974. There was no warning when the soldiers came one early morning.

They surrounded the village while others moved from homestead to homestead, waking up people and ordering them to load their belongings into army lorries.

Although people knew that something would happen soon when the army started erecting the fence, electric poles and then connected electricity, nobody knew when exactly whatever was going to happen would happen.

A few days before the people were headed into the keeps, the soldiers came to close our school and all other schools in the area. After closing down the schools, the soldiers closed down all shops and grinding mills. Then they called for a 12-hour curfew.

All this happened a few weeks after a detachment led by Kid MaWrong-Wrong came into the area.

There were so many stories about the two comrades. Some people said the two could split into several people. Others said these two could just disappear into thin air. We were also told that the bullets would bounce off them.

I am not sure, *Mama*, if Kid MaWrong-Wrong's detachment is the one that hit a road construction site at Bellrock, east of this village. We heard thunderous sounds one morning. Since we were young, we thought the sounds were coming from the mines in Bindura, where they detonated dynamites.

But word travelled fast. It is not clear how Ahefa got the news. Within minutes, the news was everywhere in the village. At the time, we were preparing for school. You remember mama whispering to us that the war had come when we were about to leave home.

'Do not answer questions from strangers,' you warned us.

'Do not leave the company of other children from the village. Do not stay behind at school. Do not talk about what you hear from the elders.'

A white man came into view just where the gravel road curved on our way to school. He had no shirt, and he had blood all over his body. He also had no shoes. He only had white shorts.

He ran past us without turning.

Muchaurawa, one of the funniest boys in the village, ran after him for a few paces and stopped when Batsirai called him back.

'My father said we should not tease strangers,' Batsirai said.

'What stranger?' Muchaurawa asked while walking back.

'Can't you see that he is a soldier?' that was Batsirai again.

'So what?' shot back Muchaurawa.

Tsitsi, Ahefa's niece, spoke about the booming sounds from Bellrock.

'The war has come,' she started.

Tsitsi spoke slowly as if she was not sure of the following words. But this made us wait and listen.

'My aunt said that vakomana have attacked a road construction site at Bellrock,' she told us.

'What is vakomana?' asked Muchaurawa.

'*Ma*-comrades,' Batsirai said. 'Don't tell me that you don't know that the freedom fighters are called vakomana?'

Muchaurawa shrugged his shoulders.

'They burnt graders and caterpillars. They also killed some soldiers there,' continued Tsitsi as if she had not been disturbed.

'That soldier survived then?' asked Muchaurawa.

'Maybe,' said Tsitsi.

At school, the older boys spoke about how the *vakomana* would disappear or stand there while bullets rain on them.

The soldiers came to our school the next day, mama. It was after break time. They moved from classroom to classroom, ordering everybody to go to the assembly point.

All the teachers were asked to line up against a classroom wall. Soldiers were surrounding the school. There were soldiers in the gum tree plantation. There were more soldiers down in the school garden. Others were sitting on top of their ugly trucks that appeared to be hungry for human flesh.

Some were smoking lazily while looking at the older girls. Their eyes lingered all over as if they expected something to emerge from nowhere. The headmaster was in his office with three other soldiers.

We waited in silence for about 20 minutes at the assembly point. We were all dead quiet. When the headmaster emerged, the soldiers were flanking him. There were all muscular white soldiers carrying heavy guns. They also had canisters and several other tube-like items dangling from their waists.

They led the headmaster to the podium. We watched this in fear. This was the third time we were so close to white people in a few days. Of course, we knew about Dr Watt, who spoke Shona. Dr Watt from Howard Hospital visited Rosa Clinic every Wednesday for special cases. He had long ceased to be a white man to the villagers. These were different. They did not smile, and their eyes darted everywhere. They kept their guns ready.

Once on the podium, the headmaster said: 'We have visitors. I am asking you to listen carefully to what they will say.'

He then stepped down, and one of the white soldiers mounted the podium. His blue eyes scanned us for seconds, and then he put down his gun.

'I am here to inform you that we are closing this school indefinitely,' he said.

We remained stone silent.

He turned to the headmaster and asked: 'Do they understand English?'

'Some of them do,' the headmaster said.

'Can you translate then?' the soldier asked.

The headmaster came closer to him. Again, the blue eyes swept across a sea of black faces.

'I want to inform you that we are closing this school until further notice,' he said again.

The headmaster then translated.

Ndoda kuzivisai kuti tiri kuvhara chikoro.

'The war has come to your area…'

The headmaster translated.

Hondo yauya mudunhu rino…

'The government is sorry that it has come to this…'

The headmaster translated.

Hurumende ine hurombo kuti ndopazvasika apa…

'But the government has no choice under the circumstances…'

The headmaster translated.

Asi hurumende haina zvaino gona kuita kana zvadai…

'The terrorists are in this area. They are our enemy. They are your enemy…'

The headmaster translated.

Magandanga vari mudunhu rino. Imhandu dzedu. Imhandu dzenyu…

'For us to keep you safe and to flush out the terrorists, we have to close the schools…'

The headmaster translated.

Kuti tikuchengetedzei zvakanaka nekuti tiione magandanga, tiri kuvhara zvikoro…

'From here, you must go back home. Don't go into the bushes because my soldiers are out there…'

The headmaster translated.

Kubva pano, munofanirwa kuenda kumisha yenyu. Musaende mumasango nokuti mune mauto…

Since we had been ordered to take all our books from the classrooms, we left the assembly running back home.

When we got home, my uncle from Bare, some 70 or so kilometres from our village, was sitting under the mango tree with my father.

We were summoned to where the two were seated. We greeted uncle, and then father ordered us to sit down.

'They have closed the schools,' Shepherd said.

'We have heard,' father said.

'It is because of the war,' uncle said.

'A lot of things will change,' father said.

It seemed as if uncle was telling father about some bad incident the previous night in another village in the north.

'So, they cut the chief's lips?' father asked to set uncle off.

'They did,' uncle said. 'They found him with a gun and a transmitter radio.'

'How many are they?' that was father.

'Two or more. But I saw two of them,' uncle said.

'Are you telling me that only two people are causing all this havoc?' father asked his mouth wide open.

'I am not sure. People are talking about miracle people. A woman said that when she prepared food for them, she just saw hands stretching out, reaching for food,' said uncle.

'She did not see the people?' father asked.

'That is what I heard. Nobody knows what exactly is happening,' said uncle.

Do you remember, *Mama*, that several things happened in the next three days before we were taken into the keeps. The war edged closer home.

There was a fierce battle at Gonhi Hills. These were greyish hills that bordered the farms and the villages – tribal trust land as they were known.

We heard the stuttering of guns early one morning. Then later, a convoy of trucks with tents covering the back drove past here.

Before noon, the story had spread about how just two vakomana had wiped out all the soldiers.

Nobody ever got to know precisely what happened on that day apart from what the people said. But one thing was certain, a lot of soldiers died.

One morning, we found that an army camp had been set up in the fields just before Rosa. There were tents and trucks and a makeshift fence. Some of the soldiers played volleyball early in the morning, while others patrolled the camp's perimeter.

Then *Mudhara* Simeon, the headman, was summoned to the camp. When he came back, all the villagers were ordered to gather under the tree that used to be here at this bus stop.

This time, a black soldier addressed the people. He was a tall young man, who spoke with an accent, which my father said was *ChiManyika. VaManyika* is the term used to describe people from Manicaland.

He told the villagers that there would be a daily curfew from dust until noon the next day for people, cattle, goats, and sheep.

All vehicles, including bicycles, and buses, he said, were banned from running during the same time and that all dogs were supposed to be tied up 24 hours a day or they would be shot.

He prohibited people from going or being near the high ground and that those who defied this risked being shot. The herding of cattle, sheep and goats was done by adults in the afternoon when children under 16 were supposed to be indoors.

Life in the village ground to a standstill. The nights were quiet, and even dogs seemed to know that danger and death lurked out there.

When the moon was full and riding the night skies, we stayed indoors instead of running around playing games.

Families never stayed up until late. If they did, then they had to be whispering to each other in the darkness of their houses. Meals were cooked early and eaten early.

The nights became longer. Sleeping became uninteresting. The August windy weather did not help. Every sound stirred up by the wind was so evident in the night.

There were times in the middle of the night when gunshots could be heard in the distance. In the beginning, we would cling to each other in fear. However, we got used to and could sleep even when the gunshots were close by.

Although people were free to roam around during daytime, most never ventured into the mountains or the hills. None dared go deep in Burutsavana or wander along rivers.

Visiting each other became a calculated move during daytime because the soldiers were on patrol everywhere.

Muketiwa was the first victim of the curfew. He was shot while walking about in the village. The soldiers announced early one morning that they had shot a terrorist. It turned out that it was Muketiwa. He had a mental problem.

His mother, Ahefa, was not allowed to bury him. The soldiers took Muketiwa's body away. His death as a terrorist was announced on my father's radio.

The word terrorist was new to us. We wondered how and why Muketiwa would be a terrorist when he had always been there in the village. We knew Muketiwa as the man who would swart imaginary flies from his mouth. He always had a cloth tied around his neck and covering his mouth. He rarely spoke. Muketiwa was always there as far I can remember.

We grew up seeing him walking about. He never bothered anyone. And no one bothered him. Even the village dogs never bothered him.

There was a time when we were afraid of Muketiwa. There were times when he would just walk about the village in a trance. His eyes would be wide open, focusing at something in the sky – something we never saw but only himself.

This usually happened when there is a new moon. I remember father saying that the moon has something to do with Muketiwa's mind. There were times when he would sit in the eaves of his mother's hut. Then there were times when he would just go and then return much later.

The day he was shot, Muketiwa was coming from Kanyemba through Burutsavana forest.

We heard the gunshots just after sunset. The sound was picked up by the caves in Nyota hills and then sent echoing throughout the villages. The dogs started barking hysterically, looking for places to hide.

There were three or four bursts of gunfire. The caves in Nyota hills echoed every burst.

After a while, two army rucks left the camps below the village and drove into the Burutsavana forest. When the trucks returned, the soldiers were singing jubilantly.

The shooting to death of Muketiwa marked the beginning of the war in this village. We rarely experienced death those days. Death was so rare that when it happened, everything ground to a stop.

During those days, children were not allowed to see the bodies of dead people. They were not allowed even to attend a funeral wake. We heard about death, but we were not allowed to get close to where it was. Whenever there was a death in the village, which was very rare those days, all children were relocated to a distant homestead.

The situation got so intense that even herding cattle during the daytime was a hazard. Well, for elders, it was a hazard, but for us, it was a blessing in disguise because all the sugar cane in the gardens were free for taking.

Ahefa had one of the biggest gardens in the village. The sugar cane grew tall and thick like tree branches. It would not have been easy for us to creep into her garden and harvest the sugar cane during any other time.

It took the war to surround us to have unlimited access to her garden at the mouth of the stream.

August used to be a slow month, *Mama*. The land was hot, and dust rose everywhere from the cleared land.

The fields were empty. We would let the cattle wander unattended. August used to be the time for ceremonies. These were traditional ceremonies, where people welcomed the dead back into their homes. August was a time for drums.

And Mutarangoma village was known for these ceremonies. In fact, the name Mutarangoma came from the villagers' love for the drum. Mutarangoma is a small village sandwiched between this village Gatsi and Damiso.

Between our village and Mutarangoma was the Munwahuku stream. People from Mutarangoma had their gardens dotted along the stream.

August was a month of plenty. There was plenty of food. There was plenty of water. There was plenty of happiness. There was also plenty of time to do nothing.

August used to be the month when we trapped mice. As young boys, we would set the traps at sunset and check them early the following day when the ground was wet and cold from the nights. Most of us had cast-away khaki jackets with deep pockets for carrying the mice.

We cleaned the mice first by removing their intestines before cooking them in salted water.

When the water dried up in the pot, the mice were transferred onto a flat tray and left to dry in the salt beside a fire.

Those of us who were crafty enough to catch a lot would sell some of the mice to the people on Chemakura. There were champions known for trapping mice. Those who drank at Kilala's also loved eating salted mice.

August was the month of the big round moon. It was the month when young people from different villages would meet for various games.

I know of boys and girls whose courtships were made possible by the big round August moon. This was the month of clear skies.

During the day, we would spend time by the river, bathing or swimming. This was when older boys would show off the size of their manhood. They would lie on the rocks, naked, just for us to admire them.

There were times when the older boys would compete to masturbate to show that they could impregnate girls. Some of the boys would even show off when they had contracted a sexually transmitted disease.

There was nothing to be scared of because sexually transmitted diseases showed that the older boys had been laid. For most, it was like an initiation. Of course, most would end up at Sekuru Ranziroti for the big bottle.

The big bottle was a 750ml bottle filled with an assortment of roots and insects floating in the dark brown water. The older boys would proudly drink this concoction and show it off to us. It worked because, after a few days, the sores on the manhood would start drying up.

In August, it was also when we would pay Maina to peep under her dress. Maina was a middle-aged mother of four who had emerged from nowhere. She was staying at her late mother's homestead.

Most, if not all, the older boys who ended up with swollen penises and crotches would have come from Maina.

They never admitted to this because Maina was known to take in every man as long as there was money. During daytime, however, when Maina's customers waited for the night, she would invite young boys to pay so that they could peer between her legs.

Nixon took me there one day. He had a few cents and did not want to go alone. He invited me, and I went along. Maina was, by village standards, a coloured. She had long, smooth legs, and she wore short dresses.

She was sitting on the door step when we arrived.

'Hey,' Nixon said.

Nixon was bigger for his age. He could, therefore, pass for a teenager, although he was just 11 years old at the time.

'Hey,' Maina said.

'We have come,' Nixon said, looking around.

'How much do you have?' Maina asked.

Nixon took out some coins and showed them to Maina.

'How much is that?' Maina asked again.

'Five cents,' Nixon said.

'Five cents?' Maina asked.

'Yes, five cents,' Nixon said.

Maina looked at me. I looked away, sweating.

'How much do you have?' she asked me.

I looked at Nixon and then at Maina.

Nixon then produced another five cents.

'This is his money,' he said, handing me the money.

'That will be one minute for each of you,' Maina said.

Nixon looked at me and said: 'It's okay.'

She reached out for the money, and we gave it to her.

Nixon knelt, and I also knelt.

'I will count,' Maina said. 'I will count up to 10, and then you know your money is spent.'

She then parted her legs slowly while counting. I could see the red lace pant and the silky-smooth thighs. She opened and closed her legs seductively.

Before I had taken in everything, she had counted to 10.

I became one of Maina's regulars from that hot August afternoon. Such escapades were not for discussion at the river, especially after Nomore had declared himself the permanent lover. Nomore had just returned to the village from the farms where he worked.

Nomore was fearsome and easily provoked. There were times when he would look for trouble. He almost killed Nicholas over Maina when he beat him up with a log and left him for dead.

August was such a month. It was the month the keeps came alive when about 60,000 villagers were driven in like cattle.

The August of the big round moon died the morning the soldiers came and bundled us and dumped us in the keep on the open where the headmen, together with some soldiers, allocated pieces of land for people to start erecting structures.

It was one huge swoop on all villages. There were 13 villages that were dumped in keep 15. More villages were headed into Keep 16 at Bellrock; others in Keep 17 at Kanyemba; and 18 at Kanhukamwe, and 19 at Musarara. Gweshe was Keep 20, and Nyachuru was Keep 21.

I remember you, *Mama*, using blankets to put up a makeshift structure for the night. All women – you, my aunts, and sisters – slept in one makeshift structure, while my father, uncles, and boys slept in another.

During the day, the elders would hurdle together, talking in whispers, while the women were busy preparing food. It was fun. It was scary. There was fear over the land.

Nobody knew why the people had been driven into the keeps.

'We are sitting ducks,' one of the village elders said. 'They can send planes to drop bombs here when they cannot fight the comrades.'

'Hitler did the same with the Jews. They were driven into concentration camps where they were gassed and killed,' another elder said.

Of course, teacher Jonga told us about Hitler later one day. He described him as the worst humankind has ever produced. He said Hitler killed more than six million Jews.

'We are finished," said another elder.

Such was the fear over the land. The elders were afraid of the future. This was evident in their eyes and gait. The future held the unknown.

For us children, it was fun to have all our school friends in one place. Since the fence surrounded the school, classes resumed. It was a short walk to school.

Life too changed. We had to dig toilets and build houses. Dusty roads separated the villages in the keep. Some loudspeakers played music all day long or broadcast news. Later, potable water was provided too.

It was a new life.

The gates to the keep were opened every morning, and people had to go out to work their fields or tend to their cattle. At six in the evening every day, the gates were closed. The district assistants stayed in a camp.

Adults were issued with some wooden pegs on which their names, village, and ID numbers were written.

There was a big board in the guard room by each gate. One had to use the same entrance to go out and enter the keep. They had to leave the peg with the district assistants on the way out. These were then inserted under a person's name on the board.

If you go out and never come back, the district assistants knew because your peg would still be there. If one was going to Salisbury or some other place for days, they had to inform the district assistants how long they would be away.

The pegs were also used to know who went out every day and when they came back. All the adults had yellow bangles they wore all the time.

At keep 15, the camp where the district assistants stayed had an earth wall, and the barracks were in a dug-up area. There were places where sentries kept guard all day and night long.

Shops opened too. Delivery trucks from Harare brought supplies to the shops. Chemakura drove through the keep to Bellrock and then Shutu before going to Shopo.

Weeks after being dumped into the keep, August slowly gave way to September. There was the smell of rain in the air. September was the month of the first rains, the bumharutsva.

It rained a lot those days. God still loved this land. It rained, and the rivers would overflow. It rained all night long. It rained, and the ground became soft.

The grass grew tall and green and thick. The cattle got fatter and shiny. The cows gave and every morning before going to school, we milked them since the kraals were close by the keeps. The fields turned to a lovely green. The gardens, too, wore a green coat.

The rain was why this land of Chiweshe was called the breadbasket of Rhodesia. The small pieces of land yielded enough to fill the silos at Concession.

The hills put on a lovely green colour while the fields slowly allowed the crops to sprout. We grew maize. There were also ground nuts and round nuts. The land gave pumpkins that needed two of us to carry them.

If what Bvanzu told me is true, all the rivers that used to flow uninterrupted are now dead. The panners have dug up the rivers in search of gold.

'There are heaps of earths everywhere,' Bvanzu said.

'The rivers do not flow anymore. Heaps of dug up earth scatter the fields. They have turned the earth inside out.'

This seems true because I can see the red earth from here, mama.

Fortunately, it never rains too much these days. The gods must be angry with the land and the people.

The land, too, seems tired and angry and punishing the people for the bloodshed and the animosity and the senselessness of it all.

There is a palpable fear today as it was then when September came with the rains and winds and thunder and the rumblings on the horizon.

Slowness and laziness are holding this land back.

The fear of September of '74 was different. It was not about the heavy rains gathering on the horizon. The fear then was of the unknown tomorrow. It was the fear of aeroplanes coming to bomb us in the keeps.

So, because of the rains of that September of '74, families worked hard to erect pole and dagga huts, which they thatched. Nyota Hills became the first victim of the keep. The hills were stripped bare within weeks.

The keeps took shape. Grey roofs sprung everywhere, and everything started to fall into place. The shops, schools, and clinics were opened inside the keep.

We started going to school, and life went back to normal. After school, we would go out to the fields or relieve those who would be herding cattle.

For some weeks, we forgot about the war. After all, we were protected, insulated from it all. Nothing would touch us here. We even forgot about the comrades.

There is nobody today as I stand here, *Mama*. I am not sure if people are watching me standing here. Apart from the heat rising with the day and the sounds of the crickets, all is quiet.

If it were in back in the days, I was growing up here, the drunkards at aunt Kilala's (Clara's) homestead would have rushed to welcome me. And ask me questions about the city. At the time, the city was called Salisbury.

Of course, this changed to Harare after independence. And Salisbury was a mystery. The villagers respected anyone from Salisbury.

Today, this is not the case. Where Aunt Kilala's homestead used to be is a heap of rubble. Her gum tree plantation bore scars from fires over time. I recall one time when Aunt Kilala brought some strong beer from Mozambique. It was called *vhinyu*.

That beer was so strong that most men who drank it could not walk back to their homes. Not only did they fail to walk back home, but they also left their waste scattered at aunt Kilala's homestead when they managed to shuffle their feet back to their homes.

Of course, they came back for some more. Aunt Kilala had a plan for them then. She had to secure their trousers by tying on the ankles before selling the beer.

The drunkards obliged, and they got drunk again such that they could not do anything but defecate in their pants. This time, they staggered to their homes with their loads of shit trapped in their trousers by the ankles.

It was a long time ago. That was a few years after independence. As I stand here, I do not see anyone to ask if aunt Kilala is alive. She also had some sons.

One of them would steal rabbits from Kamukwasha's homestead and then go to the veld by the stream. Once there, he would set the rabbit free and set his dogs after the animal. The dogs would then catch it, and the boy would display the rabbits as if he had found them in Nyota Hills.

There is now a row of houses along the stream where aunt Kilala's son would perform his con act and where we used to herd cattle. I can see the houses from here. Their zinc roofs are gleaming in the heat of the sun. It also seems that the heat is lighting flameless and smokeless fires that rise like a mirage.

The row of roofs is like a stream of white water that pours into a broader and bigger white pool further down. I reckon that the larger pool is now where Rosa Township is.

There seems to be more buildings now than the two shops and a rural council bar that used to be there.

The bar used to be an oasis of fun and joy back then. When independence came, a group of Zanla comrades came into the area.

I remember those days because the Four Brothers had just released a hit song – *Makorokoto*.

The comrades set up camp in the old building that once housed the grinding mill. Somehow, as children, we would assemble at this 'camp' where the comrades played music, drank, danced, and exchanged girls. Nobody complained because the memories of the war were still very fresh.

Of course, the comrades left several girls with children. The comrades disappeared later. I am not sure after how long. But they disappeared, and life returned to normal.

I wonder if the bar is still in the same place where every Boxing Day people would meet to watch fights. This happened for years before the war and soon after independence.

Christmas in the village was real Christmas. Rosa Township was the place to go to show off our new clothes. I know brothers who met sisters on many days, and they later settled down. I also know of others who died on such days because of various causes.

One fight I still remember was between this giant who used to be the security guard at the bar. He was a fearsome man who wore a greenish uniform. If I am not mistaken, he wore size 13 shoes. Even then, his feet seemed to rebel in the biggest size I have ever seen in my life.

He moved around the bar, making sure that no under-18 boys sneaked in. He also made sure that anyone causing trouble would be thrown out. Indeed, he had the muscles to yank up men as if he was yanking up dolls, dangle them to the gate where he would dump them.

Nyamukonda was his name, I recall now. He would also grab mugs of beer and sip. He called this 'kubvisa huroyi' (a sign that the beer is safe to drink). Although many people pretended to be happy about this, the truth was they could not stop him.

Makirosi was a slightly built man who had been to jail several times. He came from behind this hill with a big rock sitting on its top. Beyond Makirosi's village is Musarara and Nyachuru, where Howard Hospital is. From there, lay farms. After the farms, the Mvurwi area takes over.

Tsimenhurike is not like Nyota. Tsimenhurike sits like a tired old woman. When we were growing up here, there was talk that another smaller rock that used to be on top of the one that sits on top of Tsimenhurike had disappeared.

Those who spoke about it in hushed tones claimed that this rock travelled to Murewa. I am not sure whether anyone believed this because Murewa is on the other side of the country and for a rock to travel there without leaving rolling marks was incredible. We believed it as children but later on, doubted it.

I recall that Makirosi's village had a bad reputation, and whenever we met boys from that village either at the dip tank or in the small hills of Chemakunguwo, we ran away. We feared them, especially since our community was considered one of the most peaceful. There were a lot of Christians in our village.

Makirosi had just been released from jail as part of an amnesty to mark independence. He and other boys from his village were at Rosa Township for the Boxing Day celebrations. It had rained on that day.

It used to rain every Christmas or Boxing Day when I grew up here. The rain, however, never stopped us from enjoying the day with pomp and fanfare. For most of us, the two days were the only days when we had tea and a lot of bread. It was also the only time when every home would open doors to every child in the village.

After playing beggars, we walked from homestead to homestead, asking for food and money. We headed for Rosa Township in the afternoon for more fun.

The bar brawl had reached the gate when we arrived on this particular day. There was one of the largest crowds ever on the day.

My cousins – Shepherd and Dickson – and I ran and squeezed our way to the front.

Nyamukonda was driving Makirosi outside using his baton stick. Makirosi had his shirt sleeves rolled up and was fuming.

While Nyamukonda was lashing unthinkingly, Makirosi was bobbing like a rubber ball. He had his fist tightened. His feet barely touched the ground as he ducked and dived. He never took his eyes off Nyamukonda and his barton stick.

The crowd was yelling and clapping. This was not going to be a balanced fight, we thought. Nyamukonda had it under control, we also thought, because he was driving Makirosi out.

We expected Nyamukonda to lunge and swing at Makirosi when they neared the gate.

Even Nyamukonda himself thought he had it under control. But when they reached the gate, Makirosi circled Nyamukonda, returning to the bar.

He waved at Nyamukonda and dared him to strike. This angered Nyamukonda, who rushed blindly at Makirosi, arms wide and baton ready. This was when Makirosi moved in and struck. It was a kick between Nyamukonda's legs.

The baton stick fell as the giant bent to protect his crown jewels. I must be honest; I never saw what happened from that moment until Nyamukonda hit the ground. I just heard a loud thud on the wet ground.

The crowd went silent, and then one drunkard shouted:
'Nyamukonda has fallen!'
Then, many voices joined in the shouting.
'Finish him off!'
'Cut his balls off!'

But Makirosi just stood there, watching. Nyamukonda lay in the wet mud like a castrated bull. His greenish uniform was soaking wet. One of his giant-sized shoes had come off. The sock was torn.

The mob moved in. The crowd spat and swore and cursed. Still, Makirosi did not move. He watched as if he was not there.

He then walked away, and the crowd created a way out for him. He returned to the bar and sat, drinking as if he had not set a new record. We walked away, leaving Nyamukonda lying in the wet mud. His greenish uniform went. There was mud in his hair.

'He is dead!' someone shouted.

'Makirosi has killed Nyamukonda!'

We heard later that Nyamukonda survived, but he disappeared without bidding goodbye to the people he had bullied for a long time.

Almost 30 years later, this place has changed so much that I wonder if people still fight because it is Boxing Day. I also wonder if Rosa is still the same.

And that hospital? The clinic, they call it. Growing up here, we never called the clinic by its name – Rosa – but by the name of the male nurse who had been there as far as I can remember.

His name was Ndawana. So, we called it *kwa*Ndawana, meaning at Ndawana's. My mother would often scare me by saying she would take me to *kwa*Ndawana's. Most of us were so scared of Ndawana because of the injection whenever a mother said we would shrink and behave.

I read about gold being found along the Munwahuku River. I know that place very well. We herded cattle there and played football. There was never gold at the time.

Just where did the gold come from later on? It was too good to believe, but most youth born after I had left made money from panning.

I hear too that they are still making money here from the gold. But wait, *Mama*, wait. There were abandoned mines near Munwahuku River. Do you remember them? And some heaps of earth and cement slabs were machines stood. There were also holes, which we later were told were tunnels into the earth. These tunnels, those how know told us, even snaked as far as under Nyota and out towards Gweshe. Teacher Jonga said the Germans owned those mines in the 1940s. He told us one day in class that the Germans abandoned the mines when Hitler was defeated. The mines are in Gombera Village. And those who are making money are from that village.

That could be why there are so many buses, minibuses and small cars running up and down all this time. There are also some motor bikes lined up over there at the junction that goes to Musarara. They seem to be waiting for passengers.

In the distance, *Mama*, Mutarangoma Hill stands like it has been forgotten by others that left in a huff. There were nights when drum sounds would be heard all night long. The name Mutarangoma comes from the love for drums.

The village Mutarangoma is not very far from this village. From here, the huts and a few modern houses with corrugated zinc roofs stand in the sun.

I never told you what happened before I left, mama. It was a few days before I left about 30 years ago, we - my uncles and cousins - visited a prophet who lived in Mutarangoma village.

We had just lost Tambudzai, Collen and Shadrack. within a week. I hope you still remember our cousins, mama. They were many, by the way.

Tambudzai was in and out of hospital, while Collen suffered what looked like a stroke at his young age. Shadrack complained of a headache two days before he was found dead. The deaths caused so much fear within the family.

It was decided that we should consult about why there were three deaths within a week.

The prophet stayed on the edges of the Mutarangoma village. His homestead was simple – two small huts with old thatched roofs. There was a pile of firewood leaning against one of the small huts.

On the edges of the homestead was an area where some aloe plants were growing. The plants were green and healthy. A row of stones marked out an area.

At the centre, close to the rocks, was a pole on which a cloth was tied. The fabric was in three colours – white, red, and green. The cloth was tearing on the edges. On the foot of the pole were three clay pots – one was full of water, the second had some stone pebbles, and the third had sand.

In apostolic lingo, such a place is called a kirawa or shrine.

Scrawny chickens were scratching the hard ground for food. There was a bony goat tied a few paces from the kirawa. The prophet was a young man. He was married to two young women. One of them acted as his assistant or interpreter.

The prophet was short and had eyes that lingered on as if they were trying to burrow deeper into your soul. He came rushing, dressed in short trousers, old flip-flops, and an old t-shirt.

It was around nine in the morning when we arrived, and the prophet attended to us an hour later. By then, he had changed into white robes. His wife, who acted as the interpreter, walked behind him carrying four doves.

The prophet said he had seen us coming even before arriving at his homestead. He also said that he had seen the problem within the family.

Then he asked us to sit in rows according to seniority in the family. The uncles – four of them – sat on the front row.

The prophet then asked us to pray while showering us with 'holy water'. He was walking around the group, his eyes searching our souls all the time.

'*Ndaona dambudziko hombe?* (I see big trouble),' he started.

'*Taurai munhu waMwari* (Speak Man of God),' we chanted back.

He mumbled inaudibly as he moved around, eyes searching.

'*Mafirwa. Vana vana.* (You lost four children),' he said.

'*Ndizvozvo munhu waMwari.* (You are right Man of God).'

'*Hapana midzimu apa.* (This is not because of angry ancestors).'

We stared at him – all of us.

'*Muri kudyanana.* (You are bewitching each other).'

Our eyes switched from the prophet to the uncles. Then back to the prophet.

'*Paita vakatakura pakati penyu apa.* (There are those among you who are loaded),' he said, pointing at the uncles.

The uncles sat; their eyes cast to the ground.'

He beckoned at his wife to bring the doves. When the doves were handed over to the prophet, he lifted them and prayed.

He put them on the ground and then pointed to all four directions with his stick.

He then said to the uncles: '*Ndichakupai hangaiwa idzi. Modzibata. Ndichanamata. Kana hangaiwa yako yawakabata ikafa, zvinoreva kuti wakaromba.*

(I will give each one of you a dove. Then I will pray. If the dove in your hands dies, it means you are not clean).'

He asked the uncles to kneel and then handed each of the uncles a dove. He started praying, and within seconds, all the doves died.

On our way back, we had to wash our hands in the water in Munwahuku.

Munwahuku's riverbanks used to have a lot of reeds. I am unsure if this is still the case now since the gold panners have raided the valley.

There used to be gardens too. Most of the gardens bristled with healthy sugar cane during the season. In some places, Munwahuku never dried up.

We never got to prove it, though that there were mermaids in places where the river never dried up.

Indeed, three boys from this village and Mutarangoma drowned at different times in one of the deeper and darker pools that never dried up.

The bodies were found washed up on the banks a few days later.

The water in that pool was still, and the eye could not see through to the bottom.

Two of the bodies were found with tooth marks all over them. Some elders who picked up the bodies later told us that one body had both ears eaten up, while the other had the lips torn apart.

Such stories kept us away from the deeper and darker pool. Later, we also shunned any other pool after the widespread talk of the mermaid.

*Ambuya va*Kachana said several girls had disappeared into the pools long back when she was a teenager only to resurface as great sangomas. One of them, she said, was *Mbuya* Nehanda's spirit medium.

Well, we never took what ambuya *va*Kachana said seriously. Like what you would always say mama, ambuya *va*Kachana added a lot of salt and spice in her stories.

It appears as if it has not rained here for years now.

The dust on the trees and the trails of smoke from the fires lit by the gold panners rise like long gum trees. All I can see from here at the bus stop are the heaps of earth dug out from the earth's stomach.

I wonder where the gold was all the years, we walked the valley herding cattle.

As I stand here at the bus stop, the sadness is returning.

Sad for coming back after 30 years. Sad for Manekaidzo, who never lived to be happy? Sad for my people whose lives never changed even after the war. Yes, sad for you *Mama*.

Sad to know that I am coming to you when you are not here. Sad too that I did not force you to allow me to come and see you in the last days.

When cancer took control of the little your life had left, mama, you asked me not to come and see you on your sickbed.

You told your brother's daughter to ask me to wait for you to die because you did not want me to see you helpless and hopeless.

Your brother's daughter told me you did not want me to know that you could not walk. Yes, *Mama*, those legs that carried you all day without rest could not do it anymore.

I hear you were so emaciated that your skin was peeling off when they lifted you to change the linen. They say you could also not help yourself.

The last time we spoke on the phone, *Mama*, you said I needed not come because you were just fine.

Although I sensed something in your voice, I did not want to argue with you.

You know, *Mama* that you taught us never to argue with our elders. But I felt the pain in your voice. You were trying just like you had always tried not to show it throughout your life.

42

But, *Mama*, pain cannot be hidden. Pain screams in silence. Pain travels distances. I felt your pain, especially when you described it.

The pain was in your stomach, you told me. You said you felt as if you were carrying it wrapped up in a wet sack. It was eating you up, you further said.

I feel tired all the time, you said. The pain worsens whenever I eat, you added.

Oh, *Mama*, I felt for you.

My stomach is bloated even when I eat a little food or drink water. I have severe and persistent heartburn and indigestion. I feel nauseous and vomit all the time. I do not eat much, you told me.

I never saw you crying, mama. Even when baba died, you did not shed a tear. You remained strong before us and carried our lives as if baba was still with us.

But the day we spoke for the last time, I felt tears in your voice. That night I researched about the pain in the stomach. I guessed right that you had adenocarcinomas.

You did not tell me that you were going to die that night. When you ended the call, you said you needed to rest, that we would talk more the next day.

We never spoke again, *Mama*. The next day, I received a call and I knew you had left.

Mama, you were always that strong woman who would always wake up to meet the day before sunrise.

I do not remember a day when the sun found you in your bed. It did not matter whether it was raining or it was cold. It also did not matter what time of the year it was.

Mama, you were always out at the same time. You had to clean the yard while humming some song whose lyrics I never got to know. I am not sure if you just hummed or it was an actual song.

It was the yard first that received a thorough cleaning. Then you chopped the wood. In the stillness of the morning, the sound of the axe rising and falling and the wood splintering filled the air.

You then lit the fire outside if it was not raining. The fireplace was at the back of the round kitchen whose grass roof sat uncomfortably on the hem of the brick wall. We had this half drum that was always on the fire. It had hot water all the time.

As we grew up, we knew without being told where to get hot water to bath. Over time, mama, it became a habit that each of us would when we saw that the water was low.

Some of the firewood, *Mama*, you stacked it against the kitchen wall close to the plate rake.

You would move to check the chickens. Do you remember that big cock that would chase people when it felt like it, mama? The cock which even Bhoki the dog was scared of?

It also gave us a tough time when you asked us to open up the chicken run for the chickens to come out. Somehow, that cock with all its huge cracked feet and disheveled feathers never threatened you, mama.

One day, I went outside to pee in the eaves of our small boys' hut where the chicken was, and you had just opened up for the chickens to come out. I could only make up a silhouette of your shape as you stood by the chicken run, and the cock was facing you.

I thought that the cock would lunge at you for some time, but after a few seconds, it sauntered off and disappeared into the fading darkness.

After freeing the chickens, you would collect some buckets and make your way to the cattle kraal on the eastern end of the homestead.

We always had a cow or two to give us milk throughout the year.

There was Manjuma that seemed to have calves all the time. Manjuma was this motherly cow that was bit and had one broken horn.

It never kicked or gave us problems. Most of the cattle we had were either Manjuma's daughters or sons. There were also her grandchildren.

We loved Manjuma. You did too, mama. If Manjuma had a calf, you would milk her and leave the rest for us. The way Manjuma looked at you, mama, seemed like you had a connection.

After milking Manjuma and any other friendly cow, you would tidy up the kitchen. There was not much apart from some clay pots that sat on some stoep facing the door.

There were three rows of such colourful clay pots. The biggest one sat at the bottom and the smallest at the top.

The fireplace was for cooking meals, and I remember there was always a clay pot beside the fire. It had maheu all the time, and they were always warm.

There was also a place for men and boys to sit on the other side. It was some raised stoep, too, but one that ran along the inner wall.

The floor was always neat, and every time you and the girls would collect cow dung to smear on the floor. The walls were plastered the white mud from the well. The kitchen had two triangular windows opposite each other.

Despite the empty kitchen, you were very proud of it and never allowed us to make it dirty. It was home, mama. You made it homely and comfortable for all of us.

You prepared breakfast. It was always porridge with milk. And if there was sugar, you made some tea for us. You used the leaves of a plant we picked in the veldt. You put the leaves on top of the chicken run to dry. Then you crushed and kept them in one of those big tins.

You wake us up then around 05h00. It did not matter if we had to go to school or on holiday. You always woke us up at 05h00, mama, like a clock, like the big cock. There was always something for us to do around the house.

Yet, mama, I could not recognise you when I last saw you in your coffin.

I never told you this, *Mama*. I did not know how to tell you about it. But do you remember the day I came back home with a broken nose, bruised knees and a swollen face?

Yes, mama. That day I lied to you that I had fallen while playing soccer in the veldt. By the way you looked at me, I knew that you never believed me. But you nodded, anyway.

You cleaned me up and nursed the wounds. Then during the night, you kept an eye on me. The nose was painful so were the knees.

I never told you, *Mama*, that I had fought three boys who called you an ugly witch. The boys from Mutarangoma confronted me on the way from school. They teased me over you, *Mama*.

They said you were a witch who was terrorising the villagers in the area. One said witches are ugly because they go into graves at night.

They spoke about your long teeth. They said your teeth are long because you eat human flesh. They said you walked bent forward because you travel long distances sitting on a traditional broom at night.

I know you had a dorsocervical fat pad. That is what doctors call it. In this village, they called it a hump. Most, if not all, people did not understand what it was.

But the boys I fought said that is where you stored human flesh. Another boy claimed you kept your snakes and owls there too.

I tried, *Mama*, not to fight like you always told me. You always reminded me that the world was not a kind place. I have never forgotten you telling me that people will always find a reason to make you feel small.

I could have swallowed anything else, *Mama*, but calling you a witch was crossing the line. You are my mother, mama. It does not matter and never mattered then what people said you did, and you were, to me, and for me, my mother.

I fought the boys, mama. It was for you. I know you knew that I lied. I saw it in your eyes.

Do you remember when baba fell sick, *Mama*? How it started like he was going to be, okay? I remember that very well.

We were preparing the field near *Kumatongo Kwa*Mudonhi. I was holding the whip while driving the oxen. *Baba* was holding the plough. You were sitting under the giant tree, selecting some maize seeds.

We could not afford treated maize seed from Bonnie's shop. You reserved some after harvesting. This was the seed you were selecting.

We were about to complete the last lap when baba said I had whipped him. I told him that I had not lifted the whip. But he said he felt like I had whipped him on the leg.

When we looked around to see if there was any insect that had bitten *Baba*, we found nothing. Then you said maybe it was a snake, but there were no tooth marks on baba's leg.

The following day, baba could not walk. The leg was swollen. You nursed him while we all thought he would get better. But the leg did not stop swelling.

Sometimes I think you and baba behaved like twins. You were both arrogant. *Baba* would force himself to walk without crutches or a stick.

Every morning *Baba* limped around, supporting himself by the kitchen wall. Then he would cross slowly to the other hut. You tried to stop him, mama, but he would give you, his look. It was the look that spoke so much without a single word uttered.

Two months later, the swelling subsided, but the leg turned charcoal black. All the veins stood out. Apart from turning charcoal black, the leg also thinned out.

One day baba told me that he could not feel his leg.

It is dead, *mwanangu*. The leg is dead, he told me.

I felt it, and it was cold and brittle. The skin was stuck to the bone.

Baba said the veins were empty of blood. He told me that he feels like things were moving in the empty veins.

A few months later, baba could not walk. He spent his last days sitting in the old wheelbarrow with wooden handles and a wheel that needed an alignment.

He died, *Mama*, *Baba*, died sitting in the wheelbarrow when we were all in the fields. You were the first to return home, and you thought he was sleeping.

I found out that *Baba* was dead when I woke him up for his meal. Even when I came back into the kitchen telling you that baba was not responding, you said maybe he was sleeping.

Yes, mama, he appeared to have been sleeping. He had a slight smile on his face. His eyes closed, and he had his hands on his chest.

I am trying, *Mama*, to imagine if you also had such a smile when they found you dead the following day after we had spoken for the last time.

You know, *Mama*, sometimes I lie awake at night. I try to put together baba's face. I know he had a white beard. It was a bushy beard that covered half of his face.

I remember he was also dark. And he had even white teeth. I hear his boisterous laughter, and I laugh along with him alone in the dark.

Mama, I also remember those moments when the two of you would take a walk in the fields below the homestead.

Baba walking in the front. He always carried his stick behind his back with his hands holding both ends. Of course, baba's back was slightly bent forward.

You would be walking behind him with your hands on your back just above the waist. *Baba* would stop and turn when he spoke to you. You would stop and listen and then say something to *Baba*.

Whenever I find myself without sleep, I wonder what you two spoke about those days when you took those strolls. I also wonder what went on in your mind when baba's coffin was lowered into the grave in the foothills of Nyota.

You know, *Mama*, what I realised recently? You froze momentarily when I told you that baba was not responding that day. I saw it in your eyes. It was this quick doubt in your eyes, and it was gone.

Strange that in times of uncertainty, such detail gets lost. But I am sure that I saw the same frozen moments in your eyes when baba's coffin was lowered, and then the grave was covered up.

You were supposed to cry, *Mama*. But you did not. I looked at you for a cue so that I could also cry. You did not. I also did not.

Later, I asked you why you had not cried for *Baba*. You said he had asked you not to cry because there was a lot you had to do. Could it be why you also said the same to me the night we last spoke? Was it what baba had told you?

I need to tell you this, mama. I did not cry when I saw your body stretched out in the coffin whose top was open. I understand now why you asked me not to come and see you when you were ill.

Your body had shrunk, and the velvet fabric that covered the inside of the coffin worsened it. You were so small that my mouth hung open instinctively when I saw you. Of course, they had tried to patch you up, but the pain still hovered on your face.

Your brother's daughter told me later that you died fighting death. Unlike *Baba*, you cried while fighting to live.

Mama, you did not lose the fight. Your life alone was one huge fight, especially after what *Baba's* brothers did to us soon after we had buried him.

I never realised, *Mama*, why you did not want me to see you in a frail state. I also did not think about why *Baba* told you not to cry. I guess now I know what it was about.

I was young, mama when *Baba*'s young brothers gathered us together three days after *Baba*'s death.

I was young but not too young not to understand what was happening. I was not that young not to see the pain and fear in your eyes.

We gathered in the big hut close to the anthill at the old homestead. I remember well how during the onset of the rain season; the anthill would breed *iswa* and *madzambarafuta*.

We fought running battles with the chickens catching the insects.

After gathering the insects, you turned them into a delicious relish. Some say that iswa is a starter, but I remember how we would clear a plateful of *sadza* with *iswa* as a relish.

Oh, *Mama*, how I miss the old homestead. There were mango trees all around the homestead. There were peach trees too. We had chickens that always disappeared into the donga we used as a toilet.

Our cattle kraal was where the sun set. We had milk all year round. Our cow Sweet always had a calf. I do not remember when Sweet never had a calf. You tended the fields around the homestead. You nursed the crops and cherished the harvest.

We had our hut as boys. The three of us shared the hut. It was behind your bedroom with baba. The kitchen faced your bedroom.

The girls' hut was close to the granary next to the kitchen. It also had its door facing your bedroom. The chicken run was close to the anthill.

We had a big yard, and during the nights when the moon was full, some children from the village came to play games. There were many games we played then until the early morning hours.

Maybe, *Mama*, you never heard this - some big girls and boys would disappear into the donga, especially when we were playing hide-and-seek. *Mukoma* Kefas used to disappear with Terezia. *Sisi* Keresenzia and Bopoto too.

At the old homestead, *Mama* was home until baba died, and his young brothers gathered us into the big old hut. I remember that morning so well, *Mama*.

You sat close to the fire just like I always remember you. We sat on the 'bench' made of mud on the other side of the hut. All us your children were in the hut. The aunts were also there.

Babamunini Charakupa did not waste time. He told you and us that we had to leave the homestead. He also said the cattle should be shared among all other families because they did not belong to baba. He also gave us one week to make a plan.

I looked at you, *Mama*. But you sat there as if you had not heard babamunini Charakupa's ultimatum. After delivering the message, they all left.

We remained, drowning in our silence and confusion.

I was confused, mama. I am still confused. But you stood up, and said: *vanangu*, your father is not here now. You need to be strong.

You turned to *mukoma* Kefas and said: you are the oldest mwanangu. This family now looks up to you.

I was the youngest then. I was confused, *Mama*.

We grew up all those years, *Mama*, with no doubt that we belonged to the family. *Baba* loved his young brothers. He was always there for them. We also loved all our cousins. Before baba's death, it was one big family.

Baba's death undid all that. I felt as if a shelter had been stripped of its roof. And the stories started coming. *Baba* was the only child of sekuru's first wife.

His mother died when baba was not even 10 years old. *Baba's* biological brother died from what could have been poisoning. *Baba* and the biological brother had eaten some green maize they cooked in a tin picked from the rubbish dump.

Baba, too, could have died but survived after he vomited everything. His brother - Shadrack - yes, mama, I remember uncle's name now - Shadrack - was not so lucky like *Baba*.

Baba and his young brother stayed alone after the death of their mother - ambuya. *Baba's* father was a drunkard who did not care much about the boys.

And *Baba* had to look after his young brother before he turned 10.

After *babamunini* Shadrack's death, baba had to go and live with his mother's people. During that time, his father - *sekuru* - married a second wife.

Babamunini Charakupa was the second eldest child in the extended family.

When *Baba* was alive, all this was hidden. To be honest, *Mama*, I never felt like an outsider. I also never thought those cows that gave us milk all year round were not ours but belonged to the family.

Baba looked after them on behalf of the family as the oldest son.

The old homestead belonged to babamunini Charakupa's mother - my step-grandmother.

Ambuya, *Baba's* mother, had no homestead when she died. I am told sekuru moved the family from the other homestead when he married the second *ambuya*.

Baba only joined the rest of the family when he was already married, and my four siblings had already been born. When he came back, the second ambuya accommodated him.

Baba was the only one at home when the second ambuya died. Her biological children were away in town.

That, mama, is how I later knew why the old homestead was not ours. I also learned why babamunini Charakupa threw us out as if we were not part of the family.

The cattle were part of a herd from *sekuru*'s sister's husband - baba's aunt. Her husband had called her a witch, and the children gave the cattle as an apology on their father's behalf.

Baba looked after the cattle - they were two initially - until the herd grew to more than 30.

You never told me this, *Mama*. *Baba*, too did not tell me this. I am not sure if my siblings knew about this.

Maybe you are surprised, *Mama*, how I got this - one of the women from baba's mother's family told me. She grew up with baba. They stayed in the same house.

Sometimes death, *Mama*, is not an end but the beginning of a whole new life. *Baba*'s death was just that.

I do not know who should I miss most - you, *Mama* or *Baba*. Sometimes I am torn between profound love for baba. I think about him a lot.

When I was a small boy, *Baba* would carry me on his broad shoulders. He sang while I hummed along because I could not make out the words.

My small legs dangled on his chest as he walked and sang while ensuring I would not fall backwards. *Baba* was my shield. He did not only carry me on his shoulders, but told me a lot of stories.

I remember when it rained while we were in the fields near the gum tree plantation. *Baba* took off his shirt and covered me against the rain. We huddled together under the tree.

The rain wetted *Baba's* broad shoulders, but he just sat there, covering me with his massive arms.

Today whenever I think about *Baba*, that day he covered me with his shirt while he exposed himself to the rain comes into my mind.

I vividly recall baba's feet digging into the wet ground. They were wet, and the water flowed around baba's feet. The rain that turned into water made some rivulets. Some of the water flowed down baba's wet trousers. This water hit the ground in huge drops that left small dents.

It rained for about two hours. All that time, baba sheltered me while the rain pounded on him, and I was comfortable. Baba was my friend. He never beat me or shouted at me.

But when *babamunini* Charakupa asked us to leave the old homestead, my feelings for baba changed. I had dark feelings because I blamed him for what happened. I blamed baba for not telling us about all that I later heard.

One day, I was so angry that I burst out about the anger building in me. We were making bricks for the new homestead. We had identified a place in one of the fields in the veldt. You still wanted us to make some more bricks, but I was tired.

I asked why baba did not tell us about his life? I wanted to know why baba did not prepare us for what we were going through. I said his brothers hated us so much that they shared the cattle and never gave us a single herd.

But, *Mama*, you did not show any emotions. You kept mixing the soil and water as if you did not hear my rantings. The others, too, just looked at me.

I went to sit at the well where I spent time throwing stone pebbles in the water and marvelling at the waves that broke each time

I threw a stone. It was like watching baba's death causing waves in my life.

I have never forgotten baba. I try to recreate his face, but all that I get is the white beard. I feel his presence, though, like this protective shadow that hangs around me all the time.

The shadow is like his massive arms protecting me against the rain.

Strange, *Mama*, that I used to speak to *Baba*. We laughed together, but I could not hear his voice, no matter how much I tried now.

As for you, *Mama*, all that I see when I think of you is the velvet cloth on which your shrunken body lay.

I have to confess, mama that I was so scared to look at your face longer than a minute. I was afraid I would cry.

I must also admit that my eyes watered when the women in the hut forced me to sit next to your coffin when I listened to them singing one of your favourite church songs.

They kept me sitting while they danced around me. And some of them started crying, *Mama*. I felt weak.

We hit hard times when babamunini Charakupa drove us from the old homestead. It took a great toll on you, mama. You had to fill in baba's shoes and then look after the six of us.

You did, *Mama*. You drove us with love to clear the ground for the new homestead. Then you led us in making the bricks. I was difficult, yes, *Mama*. I was because difficult because I guess it was age then. I did not understand life.

But you told us that we were creating a new life. You said we were building our homestead, which no one would claim as theirs.

We have hands, you said, and they would not perish just by making bricks.

We worked, *Mama*, and sang as we moulded the bricks. Sometimes we went the whole day without food. Drink water, you would say, drink water *vanangu*. There will be food in the evening.

And we drank water. There was also food every evening.

And you sang for us. We sang together. And we worked, mama, while we sang. I remember that this was your song all the time. Even baba once sang along with you while working in the field close to Munwahuku stream.

Mama, you always put up a brave face before us. I always wondered how you managed to do this until one morning when you cleaned up the yard. I woke up to go and pee behind our new hut at the new homestead.

I saw you standing facing the east. Your head was bowed, and you were talking to yourself. You attended church, mama, but you were never a prayer warrior such that you could wake up to pray. I became curious and wanted to hear what you were saying.

You were talking to *Baba*.

Things are hard, you told him, but we are managing.

Vakomana are growing and very helpful except for Tafirenyika, who throws tantrums.

Tafirenyika is angry with you sometimes, although he does not say why? I guess he misses you since you used to be together always. Maybe it is age, you told *Baba*.

You told baba about the new homestead and the fields and what his young brothers had done.

I know you see these things; you told him. I also know that you are keeping an eye on your children and me.

It was as if *Baba* was near you when you spoke. I looked around to see if baba was, but I only saw your silhouette.

Mama, you loved baba, right? I never saw you kissing him or holding hands, but you loved him, right. And even after he died, you still loved him?

The other day I told you, *Mama*, that I fought some boys after they called you a witch. Those boys were not the only ones who called you a witch. Even our cousins, too, called you a witch.

I also believed all those people, but you are my mother. But, mama, that is not entirely why I did not believe them. I did not believe them because people did not stop dying after you had died.

People had been dying, mama, before you were born. People died when you were living. And, as I said, they are still dying as we speak.

I told you about Tambudzai, Collen and Shadrack. They died. They are not the only ones, *Mama*.

There is something else, *Mama*. You need to know this. Maybe you knew, but you never said anything about it. The real reason *babamunini* Charakupa asked us to leave the old homestead was that everybody said you were a witch.

Baba's sickness, mama, made people talk loudest but behind your back and our backs. *Babamunini* Charakupa's son Batsirai's mysterious short illness and death when he was 13 years old.

Musarurwa's drowning in the river when we went swimming.

Mama, are witches ugly people? I am not saying you were ugly. I saw in you a beautiful soul. You were caring and loving in your way. Yes, you were dark-skinned. You had that thing on your back. It made you walk bent forward. One of your legs was disabled.

58

I love you, *Mama*. *Baba*, too loved you. All of us, your children, love you. I am not sure if baba knew about what people said about you. But for us, your children knew it and still know it. Our cousins knew and still know it.

When baba died, and you did not drop a tear, people spoke about it. They did not know why you acted strong, mama. Our relatives were convinced, though, that you had bewitched *Baba*.

Babamunini Charakupa's action against us was not so much because baba was a step-brother. It was because they said you had bewitched *Baba*. They said you had bewitched Batsirai and Musarurwa.

It was an act meant to throw us out of the family. They wanted us to be outcasts, but we had you, *Mama*, to stand by us.

But, *Mama*, we also lost *Sisi* Dadirai to death. *Mukoma* Kefasi too died, mama. All of them, *Mama*, they died.

I am sure you knew about the accusations. You did, *Mama*, but you never said anything. You never spoke badly about *babamunini* Charakupa after he sent us packing from the old homestead. You still respected him and accorded him all the roles of a father to us.

When *Sisi* Dadirai was about to be married, you went to *babamunini* Charakupa to tell him about it. They all came to our new homestead when the in-laws came to ask for *Sisi* Dadirai's hand in marriage. The hut was packed with all the cousins and aunts.

Babamunini Charakupa presided over the proceedings, and we had lots of food prepared by the aunts that day.

You also did the same when *mukoma* Takaruza married. *Babamunini* Charakupa led the delegation to *mukoma*'s in-laws across the river.

You never took up any role *Baba* would have taken. Instead, you gave it to *babamunini* Charakupa.

Mama, are all witches ugly? I am just asking.

There are many things we never spoke about, *Mama*, when you were still alive. You and I saw baba dying. We also saw all the other five of your children, my siblings die.

We never spoke about this because we did not know where to begin such a conversation. For example, *Sisi* Dadirai's death caught us by surprise, mama. She had just married. She moved to her husband's village. They had a son.

Sisi Dadirai did not last a year, *Mama*. One morning, her husband's brother came on a bicycle to tell us that *Sisi* Dadirai had committed suicide. She did not leave a suicide note. None of us got to know why she killed herself.

We buried her next to *Baba*.

Once again, I watched you grieve in silence. I saw a shadow of pain on your face. But you carried it all without a word.

None of us ever knew why *Sisi* Dadirai decided to kill herself, leaving a baby like that. I was born after her. She was three years older than me. She was the one I played with. We fought as any siblings would fight. But she grew up fast as most women do. Then she married because you could not afford to keep her in school after baba's death.

There is something I want you to know, *Mama*. I believe you remember those nine rocks close to where the cattle kraal was at the old homestead. Some old bricks and a broken roof sat on the rocks.

Baba said it was a granary used by the second *ambuya*.

We do not have granaries that sit on rocks anymore these days. Back then, granaries were built of poles and dagga. The rocks were lined up.

Usually, there were nine of them. They would be lined up in three rows. A bed of mud, grass and poles were built as a floor that sat on the rocks.

The walls would be erected on the floor that doubles as the foundation. There were compartments inside the granary where maize or groundnuts were kept.

I always wondered why those rocks were not cleared. I also could not understand why whenever we ploughed close to the cattle kraal, we would go around the rocks, old bricks and the broken roof.

With time, the rocks, the old bricks and the broken roof formed an island in the middle of the field.

One day, *sahwira* Piasi saw me sitting close to that old granary. He was passing by, and he asked whether I was talking to *sekuru*.

Piasi is our family friend, *sahwira*, *Mama* if you have forgotten him. He is the one who buried you. He also buried *Baba* and all the others.

'Which *sekuru* are you talking about?' I asked him.

'Your father's father,' he said, laughing.

'*Sekuru* is dead,' I told him.

Then he said: 'That is where your sekuru died.'

'Where?' I asked, jumping up.

There where you are sitting, he said, coming close to where I was sitting.

Sahwira Piasi told me that *sekuru* committed suicide in the granary around 1970.

He also said *sekuru* and the second *ambuya* had problems. When sekuru killed himself, the second *ambuya* had left.

'Did you not know this?' Piasi asked me.

I moved away from the rocks and the broken roof.

Piasi laughed and said: 'He is not there anymore. We buried him in the Nyota Hills.'

I looked at the broken roof and then at Nyota Hills. Then at *sahwira* Piasi.

'I see you did not know this,' *sahwira* Piasi said. 'They found your sekuru two weeks later. His wife had left with all the children. People did not bother about him because he would disappear for weeks and then come back. He moved from village to village drinking.

'His dog alerted the neighbours when it barked all day and night facing the granary. When the villagers came, the smell of death greeted them.

'I helped take down the body that was just bones at the time. The granary was left untouched until it collapsed, leaving these rocks, poles, and the broken roof.

'Your sister followed your sekuru, *sahwira* Piasi said, walking away," *sahwira* Piasi said, walking away.

There is a lot we never spoke about, *Mama.* A lot.

Oh, *mama*, I may forget to tell you about the dead woman I love. She is dead, *mama*, but I love her.

She was a bit older than me when we met. She was washing clothes in the river, and I was herding the two cows *mukoma* Kefasi bought for us after *babamunini* Charakupa had taken away the others.

You remember that after *Sisi* Dadirai's suicide, we all felt the knock death brings. We had seen baba dying, but we never saw *sisi* Dadirai dying. She just died like that.

I know, *Mama*, death never ceases to shock even when we expect it. If we still feel the shock of seeing a person dying slowly, *Mama*, how about some whose death is thrown at us?

I dealt with many things at the time, *mama* —*Baba*'s death, which I saw approaching each day. *Baba* tried to be strong, but his strength dried as the pain worsened. We counted down the days. Still, his death shocked us.

Sisi Dadirai's death did not shock us, mama, but we died with her. Something in us died with her. I remember days after burying her; we found it hard to eat. I was scared of going outside during the night.

The other boys, including my cousins, did not make it easy for me. They spoke about how you, *Mama*, were eating up your children.

I almost believed them. But you are my mother. It does not matter what people say about you. As they say, one cannot disown their mother.

I stopped herding our cattle with the boys in the village. Every morning, I took our two cows to the river. While sitting on the rocks that face the river crossing from the clinic where women and girls wash clothes, I read books.

I had never seen her in any of the villages close to ours. I knew all the girls from Mutarangoma, Damiso, Majome, Kakora and Majanga. She was not from there.

One day, she crept up to me while I was reading Patrick Chakaipa's novel *Karikoga Gumi Remiseve*. *Mukoma* Kefasi bought the book for me. I did not realise her presence until she coughed. I turned, and there she was—a stranger before me.

I was 17 at the time, *Mama*. She was 19.

'Hey,' she said.

'Hey,' I said.

Then she moved closer to me.

'You like reading,' she said.

'I like reading,' I answered her.

There was an awkward moment between us. She stood there, chewing on some grass.

I sat there, avoiding her eyes. In the distance, Rosa clinic's roof shone in the heat of the day.

Our two cows were lying in the shed of the muzhanje tree, lazily chewing cud.

'What is the title of your book?' She asked.

I showed her the cover, and she looked while reading out.

'*Karikoga Gumi Remiseve*,' she said.

I nodded.

'Patrick Chakaipa,' she said again.

I nodded.

Then she smiled and said: He writes well.

I nodded.

'Have you read *Garandichauya*?' She asked.

I shook my head.

'You must read it,' she told me. 'It is more interesting than this one,' she added.

'What's your name?' She asked.

'Tafirenyika,' I told her.

'Tafirenyika,' she repeated.

'Yes, Tafirenyika,' I said again.

'Maria,' she said, stretching her hand towards me.

I stretched out mine and took her hand in greeting.

'I am new here. My parents died in a car accident. I came to stay with my aunt,' she told me.

'I was born here,' I told her. 'I stay up there close to that mountain; I said, pointing at Nyota.'

'Are you still in school?' she asked.

'I am waiting for my results. Form four,' I said.

'I am waiting to start my nurse training next month,' she said.

That is how I met Maria, *Mama*.

Baba had many stories, *Mama*. One day I asked him about how he met you. You know what? *Baba* said I should not tell you about him telling me how you met him.

I guess now I can talk about it, mama. I know you will not ask me to stop talking by looking at me like you always did.

I asked *Baba* why you were quiet and never bothered so much about what people say about you?

We were herding cattle in the veldt, and when the sun became hot, we sat under fig tree where you said I was born. There where the ants crawled over me while you fought hard to scare them away.

Baba told me that a dzangaradzimu once kidnapped you.

Is it true, *Mama*? I understand there are no *madzangaradzimu* anymore. He said that you were about five years old.

Your mother - ambuya - sent you outside during the night to collect some firewood from the pile in the eaves of the hut.

Baba said *madzangaradzimu* are so tall that you cannot see where the head is. He said they have long, thin legs.

That thing or animal, *Baba* said, took you to the world of the dead, wherever that is. You only came back one morning after months.

Do you know where the village borehole used to be, mama? In that open space where we brought the cattle every sunset before driving them into the kraals? I know you cannot forget the place because we used to play soccer there, *Mama*.

It is where they found Chasi's head when the war came to our area. Do you remember Chasi, *Mama*?

He was accused of selling out the boys - Zanla combatants – who were killed one morning behind Nyota. Those boys whose bodies were dangled by a Rhodesian army helicopter?

Anyway, *Mama*, you could have forgotten the old borehole. The pipings are still intact, but the water has since dried up.

Some villagers stripped some of the parts. It must be Cain, mama. Who else in this village strips things? Cain, of course. Did he not strip our garden's fence?

But well, *Mama*, *Baba* said they found you wandering around that open space where Chasi's head was found. There where the borehole stripped by Cain was.

For some time, according to baba, you could not speak.

He said you started making out words when you turned 10 years.

'Your mother spoke in her heart all those times,' *baba* told me. 'She talked in her heart.'

I asked him: '*Baba*, how can a person talk in her heart?'

Baba said: 'Your mother did.'

I pushed him on: 'How?'

Baba looked at me and said: 'My boy, this world is never quiet. We do not hear the sounds or the voices because we do not listen carefully.'

When baba said this, his eyes were dazed. He was looking in the distance at Gonhi Hills. Those hills, mama, were always grey.

I looked at *Baba*, and I shivered.

'Do you also speak silently?' I asked *Baba*.

He said, without looking at me: 'We all do, my boy. We all do.'

'You and *Mama*...' I wanted to ask him, but he looked at me.

'Your mother and I understand each other well. I know most people do not understand her,' baba said.

'This thing that kidnapped *Mama*, where did it take her to?' I asked *Baba*.

He said: 'The spiritual world is not for us to understand. Your mother never talks about the time she was in the world of the dead. I doubt she will ever talk about it. That is why the spirits took away her speech when she came back. Whatever she saw and did, she cannot talk about it.'

'But, *Baba*,' I asked him again, 'where did you meet *Mama*?'

Baba said: 'At the grinding mill.'

I chuckled because I could not believe people meeting at a grinding mill, falling in love and marrying later.

'Yes,' *Baba* said, 'we met at the grinding mill. Those days, the grinding mill was at Nikirosi's farm. We had to go there once a month because of the distance. Your mother lived in the village next to my aunt's where I was staying.'

Baba did not say much after that. But, *Mama*, where did the *dzangaradzimu* take you to? What did you see that you never spoke about?

This dead woman I am in love with, *Mama*, also died of cancer. You died of stomach cancer, and she died of brain cancer.

I wish you were alive to respond to me because I want to tell you that I love her.

Baba did not tell me how you two realised that you loved each other. I understand now how difficult it is to say at what point exactly one feels they are in love.

I have heard *Mama*, people talking about love at first sight and others speaking about never imagined ever being in love with the person they ended up with.

There are bizarre stories about how people end up as couples. I will never know how you and *Baba* became a couple because he did not tell me the whole story, and neither did you.

But I will tell you how I loved this woman and still kept the love long after she died. Can you believe that she married and had children and I also as you know married and had kids, *Mama*?

We both did and had kids, but even then, we felt joined here on the waist like those inseparable twins. They call them conjoined twins or Siamese twins. I guess our souls were conjoined.

I did not feel the love for her from here on the heart, *Mama*. I felt it deep down where time or arguments could not reach. And that could only be the soul.

After meeting at the river where she was washing clothes like I have told you, *Mama*, I cannot recall all the details of how we ended up conjoined by our souls. I understand baba when he could not tell me exactly how your love grew.

I have a few recollections, though, mama, about how Maria's life became mine and my life hers. I can only tell you what Maria said to me about her parents.

Beyond that, *Mama*, I have no details.

She was the only child. Her young brother died in the car accident that killed her parents. The parents were both teachers.

Do you, *Mama*, remember that accident involving the bus, Chemakura and another small car? The accident that happened the year the floods of *Bumharutsva* washed away the Ruya Bridge just before Rosa Township close to the dip tank?

No, *Mama*, the accident did not happen on the day the bridge was washed away. I am just saying that was the year it happened. And maybe, yes, because the bridge had been washed away too.

When the flood washed away the bridge, the council had to create another crossing point on Ruya.

The new crossing point was below the dip tank, where Ruya's waters were shallow. The place where we used to catch nyungururwa on our way from school. The water there was clear and clean. Small frogs swam across the river to hide in the mud on the banks.

The council workers in yellow overalls worked for weeks to create another crossing by erecting a narrow concrete bridge. Those men, mama, were lazy because they would work in the morning, cook sadza under the trees, eat and then sleep in the shade. Imagine, mama; they took weeks to erect that concrete bridge.

The council workers had to make another road from the old one to connect it to the narrow bridge. They created a bend on the road that made it difficult for drivers to see what was coming from the other direction.

I am not surprised that Maria's family died at that small concrete bridge, mama. It was so narrow that Chemakura, which appeared from the bend covered in dust, had no time to give way to Maria's parents' car on the narrow bridge.

They died, Maria told me, when we were sitting with our feet in the water one day. Tino, my brother, was on my mother's lap. He also died.

I looked at Maria, *Mama*, and she had the same stillness in her eyes as you always had. Although she spoke about how her family died, she did not shed tears.

Like you, *Mama*, Maria did not say much about many things. But she smiled a lot, and she cared for me.

She became my shelter from the boys who bullied me - those boys who called you a witch. Maria never called you names, *Mama*.

'I like your mother,' she always told me. 'She is a kind woman.'

That is how Maria made me smile. We held hands most of the time when she came to help me with the cattle. We read to each other and shared books. She had lots of books.

'My father,' she told me one day, 'bought me all these books. He wanted me to read and go to university. Now that they are dead, she added, I will not be able to go to school.'

Maria's aunt had a few goats and lots of mango trees. Before Maria came, I never had access to the mangoes because her aunt was mean.

What about your aunt? Can't she do something for you to go to university? I asked her one day.

She looked at me expressionlessly and said: My aunt would love me to go to university, but she does not have money. She is a widow, and her children never take care of her.

Maria's story was our story, mama. Her father's brother sent her to stay with her aunt because his wife never loved Maria.

'*Babamunini* took away our furniture and everything,' she said. 'He also took me to his house, but his wife and children never liked me.'

Unlike us who had you, *Mama*, Maria had no one.

She told me: 'My cousin sister took away all my clothes. They ate food while I was sitting outside if *babamunini* was away. I also stopped going to school after *babamunini* got father's money.'

Maria did not go to university, but she trained as a nurse, and I trained as a teacher.

It is a long story, *Mama*.

I almost believed the people who called you a witch, *Mama*. I did, and I did not tell you this.

I did when a car hit *mukoma* Jekiseni, and he died on the spot. *Mukoma* Jekiseni was working as a postman in Harare in the early days of Independence.

Mukoma Jekiseni died a few weeks after getting the job. Your brother's son, *sekuru* Taurai, took *mukoma* Jekiseni when he visited us.

Sekuru Taurai said he would talk to his friend who worked at the post office about a job. It did not take long before we heard that *mukoma* Jekiseni was working.

The morning he died; you did not wake up the usual time to clean up the yard. You remember that I asked you whether you were sick.

'I cannot feel my spirit,' you told me. 'It is as if someone is sucking it with a pipe,' you added.

Sisi Keresenzia had to clean up the yard and boil some water for you to bathe. That was the first time I saw and heard you complain.

At the time, mama, I did not know what a spirit was. Yes, the few times I attended Sunday school, they spoke about spirits and the soul. It was all about heaven and hell. I must admit that I never understood most, if not all, of the stuff they taught us.

They taught us about the Father, the Son and the Holy Spirit. When you told me about your spirit that day, I wondered whether it was the Holy Spirit or just some spirit.

I could not ask you because I knew you would not talk about it. Although I did not know at the time what baba told me about the kidnapping by the *dzangaradzimu*, I knew you would not talk about it.

You always encouraged us to attend Sunday school, although you were never excited about church the way *amainini mai* Tanatswa and others were.

I never told you, *Mama*, why I stopped going to Sunday school. Do you recall when you tried hard to encourage me to go, but I refused? I did not refuse because I wanted to water the vegetables with you in the garden.

I also did not refuse because I wanted to spend the day with you, mama. I love you, but I could have used a little time away from you attending Sunday school.

The news about *mukoma* Jekiseni's death came around two in the afternoon. You were still lying in the sun behind the kitchen. You always had this place where you rested. That afternoon, we loitered around the homestead as if we were waiting for something to arrive.

It was another hot August day when there was nothing much to do. The fields were empty, and the wind blew, stirring up some dust. All the hills - Gonhi, Dambatsoko, Nyota, and Tsimenhurike - were grey.

In the distance, the clinic's zinc roof shone, throwing up a pale shade of white into the sky.

From our homestead, we could see the dusty road snaking up from the Ruya towards Nzvimbo.

Whenever a car came, we saw dust rising in the air. The cattle would roam free, searching for leftover maize cobs in the fields. The chickens, too, sought shelter in the eaves of the huts.

I cannot say we stayed home that day because of mukoma Jekiseni's death. August is just a lazy month. It also made us all lazy.

There was nothing to do besides setting up traps for mice in the fields at dusk and waking up early to check if the tarps had caught mice.

The only people who seemed to have things to do in August were *Madzibaba* Philip's sons. They had that big garden in Burutsavana valley. They also had that old Bedford truck they used to transport vegetables to Harare three times a week.

Although the Bedford truck complained all the time, the boys seemed to understand it very well. We wondered how one of the boys drove while the other held a container full of diesel, feeding it directly into the engine.

The Bedford had the driver's seat, and the passenger had to squat and balance the container.

How the Bedford smoked, mama. It always left this heavy smell of diesel, engine oil and burnt tyres hanging in the air long after it had gone.

Those boys, *Mama*, remember they brought the letter from Harare. One of them came running and shouting for any one of us to meet him halfway and receive the letter.

He said that the Bedford might stall, and starting it would be another big problem.

I ran and received the letter. It was the first letter that was ever delivered to the family. I could read then. It was addressed to you, although you could not read it.

Mama, that is one thing I never understood - you always told us that education was good, but you could not read or write.

Baba, too, could not read or write, but the two of you never stopped encouraging us to go to school.

You were all waiting for me when I came back running, with the letter between my sweaty fingers.

The others crowded around me, trying to grab the letter away.

'It is *Mama*'s letter,' I told them, shrugging them away.

You sat up then and just looked while they tried to snatch the letter from me.

Then you said, let him bring the letter to me.

They followed me when I handed you the letter, and you looked at it as if you were reading it.

You turned it over and then handed it to me.

'Read it for us,' you told me.

I took the envelop, tore one end open and pulled out a piece of paper.

I read it silently at first, my lips shaping up the letters.

'What does it say?' You asked me.

The others, too, looked at me and said: What is it?

I looked at you, *Mama*. Then I looked at the letter. I did not know how to tell you.

'Who sent the letter?' You asked.

'*Sekuru* Taurai,' I said.

'What is he saying?' You asked again.

'It is about *mukoma* Jekiseni,' I said.

'What about Jeki?' You wanted to know.

'He died this morning,' I told you without rereading the letter.

I handed the letter to you and walked away.

74

My mind was filled with dark thoughts about what you had said that morning.

Yes, *Mama*, I almost believed the people who accused you of being a witch. I tried to understand how you could talk about spirits, and then *mukoma* Jekiseni died?

After we buried *mukoma* Jekiseni, I went to Sunday school for the last time. I asked the Father about the Trinity, emphasising the Holy Spirit. I also asked him what happened to the Heavenly Father's wife, the Son's mother.

The Father looked at me and said: You have an evil spirit. The devil is leading you into darkness.

I wondered at the time whether you had a good spirit or an evil one, mama. I almost believed the people who called you a witch.

I am sorry. I know better now.

Sometimes, *Mama*, I forget to say what I want because there is a lot. For example, I did not tell you everything about the Sunday school issue.

Maybe, it is because we never spoke much when you walked this earth. Apart from the night you asked me not to come. We spoke longer than we had ever done.

Silly me, *Mama*, I never realised you were bidding me goodbye. I just thought, well, that is my mother talking to her child. You know that I was always, and I am still a child to you, *Mama*. You always reminded me of that too. You did the night we spoke for the last time. That night I tried to command you to take your medicine.

'You said, ah child, now you think you can tell me what to do?'

'Yes, *Mama*,' I said, 'take your meds.'

You chuckled and said, 'you are my child, do not forget that. I know you buy the medicines; I decide when to take them or when not.'

'But *Mama*,' I tried to chip in.

'There is not but, mama, here child. You are my child—the boy I delivered in the veldt alone under the big fig tree. I fought ants to stay away from you.'

Whenever you spoke about how you delivered me, I knew it was time to change the subject.

'*Mama*,' I said.

'What, my child?'

'Are you sure I should not come to see you?' I asked again.

'Come to see me and do what? Are you a doctor now? Do you now have the power to heal sick people like me?' You asked.

I tried to smile, although I knew that you could not see the smile. Do you remember those smiles I wore when I was a child and wanted you to fry some eggs? I never liked okra, *Mama*.

Whenever you cooked okra and *sadza*, I feigned illness. I would get a blanket, spread it behind you in the kitchen and pretend to sleep.

When the sadza was ready, and others were eating, I would start groaning not out of pain but in anger. You knew what that meant, mama, didn't you?

Then you would ask *Sisi* Dadirai to go and get two eggs from the chicken run for me. You fried the eggs and asked me to sit up and eat. I had perfected my act, *Mama*.

I took time to sit up, and then I would stretch my hands for you or *Sisi* Dadirai to wash them. Even eating would be a slow and painful act, but a determined one. When I was done, I would smile, stand up and thank you sincerely.

At least you saw those smiles, but talking to you over the phone was different. But this is not what I want to talk about, mama.

It is about Sunday school - the reason I stopped going. I told you about the questions I asked. Yes, partly it was because the Father called me something like a devil or that the devil was speaking through me.

The real reason, *Mama*, was how they portrayed the devil. They drew an ugly figure of the devil—one with bloodshot eyes, fangs dripping blood and claws for nails.

The one that hung in the Sunday school classroom had a fork with red hot prongs. He was walking on top of burning bodies. There was smoke rising from what appeared to be a deep cavern.

You are my mother, and you know what my skin is like. I know you also knew how your skin was like, *Mama*. Somehow, the caricature of the devil reminded me so much about you.

The people in the village called you ugly, *Mama*. You are beautiful, mama. You will always be beautiful in my eyes. I am not saying this because you are my mother. I am saying it because that is what it is.

You had the Bible. You carried it whenever you went to church. I know, mama that you never read it because you could not read. But somewhere in that book you carried with so much respect is a verse that says God created man in His likeness or image.

I doubt God is ugly, *Mama*. He cannot be, and since you were created in his image, there is no way you could have been ugly. I take this verse says that each one of us has some godliness in them. We carry God in us. We exude God's power and purity.

I am just saying I stopped going to Sunday school because of that caricature of the devil they drew like us.

When *Baba* died, they accused you, *Mama*, of bewitching him.

When *Sisi* Dadirai killed herself, they also accused you. They also accused you of mukoma Jekiseni's death when he was hit by a car.

We have, *Mama*, spoken about these.

We have not talked about how the whole village looked at you with accusing eyes when *mukoma* Kefasi returned from Harare.

When *mukoma* Kefas left one cold June morning, he did not return until years later. He left with *Madzibaba* Philip's boys in their old Bedford truck. *Mukoma* Kefasi sat on top of cabbages and sacks of potatoes.

I always remember him sitting in the back of the old Bedford truck with his arms resting on the sideboards. He seemed not interested when you handed him some money for food and transport.

I also remember that you did not want *mukoma* Kefasi to go to Harare after *mukoma* Jekiseni's death. *Sekuru* Taurai convinced you one evening that nobody has control over death.

Sekuru Taurai said if mukoma Kefasi worked, he would help you with some money and improve our lives. You did not say why you did not want *mukoma* Kefasi to go, but I knew why. I saw it in your eyes, mama. The people would accuse you of bewitching him if he was going to die, just like *mukoma* Jekiseni.

'Vatete,' *sekuru* Taurai said, 'you need help. Look, you have him,' he said, pointing at me. 'He wants to go to school.'

You did not say anything, *Mama*.

Sekuru Taurai pressed on: 'I know how you feel about Jeki, vatete. But that was an accident. The departed decided. It was not your fault.'

You just stared at *sekuru* Taurai, mama.

'I also feel saddened by Jeki's death. I wanted him to help you around the house. You need help, vatete,' *sekuru* Taurai insisted.

You looked at *mukoma* Kefasi, who sat near the kitchen door. He had his massive head buried in his huge palms. I sat next to *sekuru* Taurai. I liked *sekuru* Taurai. He brought us food every time he visited. *Sekuru* Taurai also liked you, mama.

Although the fire had burnt out, you had a stick you used to turn the ashes over as if you were looking for something. I looked at you, *sekuru* Taurai and then *mukoma* Kefas.

I understood why you did not want him to go. After *mukoma* Jekiseni's death and baba's death, *mukoma* Kefasi was the head of the family.

You kept turning over the ashes, and after a while, you said: 'Kefasi.'

Mukoma Kefasi answered: 'Amai.'

'Do you hear what *sekuru* Taurai is saying?' You asked him.

Mukoma Kefasi released his massive head from the prison of his huge palms and said: 'Yes, *amai*. I hear him.'

'What do you think?' You asked him again.

Mukoma Kefasi' eyes were big, and they bulged as if they would roll out of the sockets at any time.

I looked at *mukoma* Kefasi. His big feet sat on the floor as if they would never carry him. *Mukoma* Kefasi had thick toes too. I do not recall him wearing shoes before he left for Harare.

Mukoma Kefasi looked from you, mama, to sekuru Taurai and said: 'I want to go. I am tired of life in this village.'

You stood up, *Mama*, and went out of the kitchen. I knew you were going to cry alone in your bedroom. The next morning, you agreed that *mukoma* Kefasi could go.

Mukoma Kefasi left, never wrote a letter or sent any money. You sometimes asked *Madzibaba* Philips' boys if they had heard about *mukoma* Kefasi.

The answer was always no. A letter came one day. It was from *sekuru* Taurai. There was some money inside and the letter.

In the letter sekuru Taurai said *mukoma* Kefasi had changed. *Sekuru* Taurai said *mukoma* Kefasi was staying alone in a different area of the city.

'This money I have sent, I grabbed from your son, vatete. I met him last week in a bar,' sekuru Taurai wrote.

I must confess, *Mama*, that I did not read this part because that could have broken your heart. I just read the greetings part and then handed you the money.

'Is that all the letter says?' You asked.

I looked at you and the letter and said: 'Yes, *Mama*. That is all.'

You took the money, but your eyes were on the letter. Although you did not say anything, I knew you realised there was something I did not want you to know.

Around 1986, *Mama Madzibaba* Philip's boys drove their old Bedford close to our home. They reversed it, and one of them came running. You were working in the garden. I was sitting in the eaves of the boys' hut, reading.

When you heard the old Bedford reversing, making that wailing noise, you came out of the garden and walked toward one of *Madzibaba* Philip's boys.

Funny that we never got to know their names. They were twins, and they looked just the same. There was Sam and Samuel. The whole village just called them Sam.

I also stood up and walked toward Sam or Samuel. Usually, if it were a letter, they would call and then I had to run to collect it. You walked toward us, *Mama*. You still had the hoe you were using in the garden in your hand.

'Where is your wheelbarrow?' Sam or Samuel asked breathlessly.

'A wheelbarrow for what, Sam?' I asked.

By then, you had gotten where Sam or Samuel and I stood.

'*Amai* Kefasi,' Sam or Samuel said, 'where is your wheelbarrow?'

We had no wheelbarrow. The one *Baba* used broke apart when we made bricks for the new homestead.

I told Sam or Samuel that we no longer had a wheelbarrow.

'What happened to the one your father used when he was sick?' Sam or Samuel asked.

'It's broken,' I told him.

'What is the problem?' You asked Sam or Samuel.

He calmed down and said, 'We have brought your son. We have Kefasi in the truck.'

'Kefas? In the truck?' You asked, dropping the hoe.

'Yes, your son Kefasi. He is in the truck,' Sam or Samuel said.

You walked towards the truck, and I followed you. *Mukoma* Kefasi was lying on his back on a heap of sacks and a blanket. We stood there, looking at *mukoma* Kefasi.

We hardly recognised him.

81

If anyone doubted that you were a witch, mama, they stopped when *mukoma* Kefasi returned home. With baba, *Sisi* Dadirai and *mukoma* Jekiseni, they spoke in whispers. Their body language showed distaste and hatred towards you.

But with *mukoma* Kefasi, they spoke openly about it. They pointed fingers and some mocked. *Mukoma* Kefasi came back bony, wide-eyed and cold. I know how cold his body was, mama because I shared a bed with him.

He could not walk, and neither could he talk. He was so weak that we had to use a blanket to take him from the old Bedford truck into the house. *Madzibaba* Philip's twin sons were so kind, mama. Maybe it was because of their faith. They helped us to carry *mukoma* Kefasi into the house. They did not ask for any payment. They said *sekuru* Taurai had brought *mukoma* Kefasi to the market where the boys were offloading cabbages and potatoes.

'We are sorry,' they said as they walked away after helping us to lay *mukoma* Kefasi close to the fireplace in the kitchen.

It was a hot day, but *mukoma* Kefasi was shivering.

You lit the fire, and I brought some more firewood. Then you made some thin porridge. There was no sugar, just salt.

I helped you lift *mukoma* Kefasi' head and place it on your lap. Then you asked me to use a spoon so that his mouth would stay open to allow the thin porridge to pass.

'He is hungry,' you said as you scooped some porridge and poured it carefully into his mouth. 'Eat Kefasi, you urged him. Eat, food is life.'

But *mukoma* Kefasi just looked at you with his glazed eyes. They were white, lifeless and unmoving. His tongue hung loosely between his teeth.

'Move his tongue to the side,' you said, 'it is blocking the porridge.'

I was shaking then, *Mama*. It was a delicate thing to do. I was scared I might inflict some injury. But you told me how to do it.

'Put the spoon under the tongue, my child. Then twist it slowly while I feed him,' you said.

We succeeded after a few trials, and *mukoma* Kefas swallowed some spoonfuls of porridge without moving any of his muscles. We gave him water, which we had to pour in slowly so that he would not choke. And you said *mukoma* Kefas needed a bath. He was lying in the sun from Harare in the Bedford truck.

While the water was heating up to bathe him, we carried him to the toilet. We used the blanket, but he could not even sit to help himself. You helped me to sit him up, and you left. *Mukoma* Kefasi' pair of trousers was ten sizes big. He used a wire as a belt. The wire was eating into his skin. I worked carefully to remove the wire and lower his trousers.

I held him from behind, my hands under his armpits. Then I lifted him to assume a squatting position. *Mukoma* Kefasi did not pee or piss.

'Is he done?' You asked.

This was a new situation, and I did not know how to respond, but you called out again, 'Is he done?'

'No, **Mama**. Nothing is coming out,' I said.

'Hold him like that for a while and see if nothing will come out,' you said.

I did not tell you that I was already tired and afraid because my eyes were trained at the top of *mukoma* Kefasi' head. His fontanelle was active. I could see it breathing.

'*Mama*,' I called out, 'nothing is coming out.'

'Dress him, I am coming,' you said.

You brought the blanket, and we carried him out into the boys' hut. You had already prepared warm water for a bath. You covered your face with a cloth when you helped me undress him and make him sit in the water. I had to bathe him.

I know I never told you this, *Mama*, but you later saw it yourself - *mukoma* Kefasi was a skeleton.

Every bone on his body stuck out. The ribs were like an unfinished reed basket. Do you know, mama, that we all have tails?

I had read about it and learnt about it in school. I saw it the first day I bathed *mukoma* Kefasi. It showed where his spinal cord ended. It was the size of my small finger.

I know you also saw this, *mukoma* Kefasi' back was soft, and the skin was peeling off, leaving open wounds. There was one deeper wound below the right armpit, it was oozing pus.

I must confess again, *Mama*, and I hope you understand that I avoided that wound. I also did not clean *mukoma* Kefas properly because it was my first time.

The next day, mama, I left you alone to clean him. I went to the river and did not come back on time. I was afraid of coming back.

I spent the day with Maria, the dead woman I still love. I told her about *mukoma* Kefasi and what the people in the village said about you.

With Maria, *Mama*, I found an ear and someone who taught me many things. I know you did not want people to know about *mukoma* Kefasi. One day I brought Maria, while you were in the garden. We sneaked into the hut where *mukoma* Kefasi was sleeping. Maria looked at him and then said, 'This is not witchcraft.'

I whispered, 'What is it? People say my mother is doing this to him.'

Mukoma Kefas did not move a bit. Maria checked his eyes and felt his pulse.

'Come,' she said, dragging me out of the hut.

We ran across the open fields towards the river. We had a place where we spent time together. It was under the trees that formed a roof but had their roots and trunks in the river.

We arrived there breathless but relieved that you had not seen us. I was relieved, too, that Maria had absolved you of witchcraft accusations.

HIV, commonly known as Aids, arrived silently. It was like the war before we were driven into the keeps. Those families that never had an affected member, looked from a distance with a disinterested look.

First there were stories in the newspapers about the new disease that had no cure. We were told that this new disease kills within six months of contracting it.

It was a disease those who know said was spread through sharing blankets, spoons, plates cups and even sitting close to people dying of it.

Then we started to hear about condoms, *Mama*. Radios and TVs carried adverts about condoms and warnings against sleeping around with sex workers. The adverts also warned against multiple partners.

For about two years since AIDS became a fear and the most spoken about disease, this village never saw anyone who died of it. Life almost returned to AIDS-free episodes when Zebedia's son returned from the city.

His name was Chamunorwa. He was working in one of the biggest banks in the city. He was much older than most of us at the time. We hardly knew him apart from his name since he built his parents the biggest house in the village. We called it the palace. The house stood on a hill slope. It had a red roof and big windows.

A few months before Chamunorwa was returned, he had started to build his own house close to his father's. He also bought two tractors that were parked at his unfinished house. A car was also parked alongside the tractors.

Chamunorwa himself rarely visited but whenever he did, the whole village would stop to marvel at his sleek car. His children never stayed in the village. They spoke English and dressed well.

His return was whispered around the village since the Zebedias were themselves a reserved lot. Although we rarely saw Chamunorwa outside, the few, including Ahefa, who visited the family whispered about his condition.

The day Ahefa came to our home, *Mama*, she told you about Chamunorwa. You asked me to leave but I did not go very far.

'He is dying,' Ahefa told you.

'Dying?' you asked.

'He is just a bag of bones,' Ahefa said. 'When he is sleeping, one sees just blankets.'

'What do they say it is?' you prodded.

'This new disease,' Ahefa said. 'It eats you alive.'

'Don't say,' you urged her.

'He does not eat. His eyes are white and emotionless,' Ahefa said.

'Does he talk?' you asked.

'Talk? How when he cannot even open his mouth? They help him to go to the toilet. He cannot walk,' Ahefa said.

'Our children will perish,' you said.

Chamunorwa died one afternoon and was buried the next day. His body, you told us mama, was wrapped up tightly so that the disease would not escape.

About four months later, Chamunorwa's wife came barely walking and was buried a weeks later. Today, their unfinished house is visible from here where I stand.

Kamukwasha's daughter was also brought back from the city and she did not last long. Then Jarata's son also. Death seized not only our village but all the surrounding villages.

I am not sure, mama, when you said 'our children will perish', you knew that one day we would be nursing *mukoma* Kefasi.

Do you remember, mama, what babamunini Charakupa said when *mukoma* Kefasi was brought home?

We were sitting outside under the eaves of the big hut, while *mukoma* Kefasi was sleeping in the sun.

Babamunini Charakupa came from the direction of Rosa township. He was not drunk that day.

'How is the unwell?' he asked, sitting on the old oil container.

'Nothing has changed,' you answered him.

Babamunini Charakupa looked into the distance beyond Rosa township. That time of the year, Gonhi hills and Bare Mountain were ash grey. The sky too was always whitish. It appeared as if the horizon was sitting on top the hills.

The roofs of Kakora Primary and Secondary schools shone in the distance. The heat rose from the zinc roofs like flames.

'I was thinking that maybe we should find out why?' *Babamunini* said.

You looked at him and then at *mukoma* Kefasi.

'What do you mean find out why?' you asked him.

Babamunini spoke with his eyes still staring in the distance.

'Why him? What happened?' he said.

'He is sick,' you said.

'Yes, he is sick. But how?'

'Many young people are sick, baba,' you said. 'It is the disease without a cure.'

'Yes, you are right, but we need to know why the ancestors deserted him? Why they failed to protect him from the woman who gave it to him,' *babamunini* Charakupa said.

You stared at *babamunini* Charakupa.

'People always die. We give birth to human beings. We know even when we give birth that one day these children will leave us,' you said.

The silence that followed your words sat heavily on us. *Babamunini* Charakupa shuffled his feet, and slowly stood up. He crossed his hands behind his back and walked away.

Of course, *Mama*, you should remember that we buried *mukoma* Kefasi two days later.

This place has so much death, mama. These eyes have seen so many people die, *Mama*. This land has eaten so many souls.

But it is our home. It is the reason we all come back to die here. Maybe death is the only thing that has not changed here. People are still dying but different deaths now.

Even the way people live has changed here, mama. From the bus stop where I am standing now, Badzarigere village is east of Rosa Township just after where the protected village was.

The huts are visible from here. I can also see a few houses with zinc roofs. Between Rosa and Badzarigere is another village called

Kamoto village. Then south of Kamoto village is Damiso and then our village. Nyota stretches from Majome village to Damiso, deep into Burutsavana valley.

Maybe you still remember Burutsavana valley during the war when Chasi sold out the detachment of Zanla comrades who were camping in Nyota Hills? That morning when we were not allowed to leave the keep and then those two helicopters came dangling two bodies.

We saw the dead bodies of two vakomana shot one early morning in Burutsavana valley. The two were part of a detachment that had just arrived in the area and contacted Chasi.

Chasi was one loud fellow who always went out of the protected village and spent the day in Nyota Hills. He would return carrying firewood and some wooden handles he would have made. Looking back now, I do not doubt that some elders knew that Chasi had contact with vakomana.

A day before the shooting, Chasi did not return home to the protected village. And the vakomana were shot the following day after Chasi had disappeared.

The bodies were brought into the protected village. They were dangling from an army helicopter that flew just above the huts. A message was being sent out through a loudspeaker for all the people to gather close to the camp where the district assistants lived.

We all emerged from the small huts and trekked to the camp while the army helicopter was hovering just above us. The bodies tied onto the helicopter were dangling, banging into each other as the helicopter circled and turned.

There were soldiers all over the place. They had guns unseen before. Most of the white soldiers had their faces painted black while black ones had veils over their faces. They watched us as we shuffled towards an open space. More soldiers sat on top of army vehicles smoking, watching, chewing gum and unsmiling.

Those on the ground herded us like cattle to the open area where we were ordered to sit on the dusty ground. I recall the deafening silence that enveloped the crowd. One could hear the feet shuffling in the dust. I am unsure if we were breathing because it was dead quiet except for the shuffling feet.

The helicopter hovered above us, and the bodies dangled. After we had sat down in the dust, the helicopter lowered the bodies and then let them hit the ground with a thud like dummies. The helicopter flew away towards the hills and disappeared.

The soldiers then ordered us to stand up and form a queue. They then ordered us to file past where the bodies were lying in the dust. They were soldiers who made sure that each one of us looked at the bodies.

When my turn came, I stood there looking down at the two men whose bodies were riddled with bullets. Their clothes had been torn. It seemed as if they had been dragged on the hard ground as shown by their torn skins. One had one shoe on while another had no shoes. They had layers of clothing.

One had his face bashed in, and both legs were broken. The other one had a twisted neck, a broken nose, and a missing eye. Both lay in the dust, broken and very dead.

Mudhara Simeon tried to walk past without looking at the bodies but was asked to kiss one of them. He hesitated, and one soldier pushed him onto the ground. *Mudhara* Simeon had no choice but to kiss the body.

The protected village gates were not opened that day. This was not new, though. The district assistants locked us up in the protected village whenever there were some disturbances in the area.

When the war intensified, the protected villages were locked up for days on end. This is what happened when the bodies were brought in that August morning. Our protected village was like a dust bowl, especially in July and August.

After viewing the bodies, we scattered to our huts in heavy silence. The narrow dusty streets were deserted that day. The nights were filled with the sounds of howling dogs and crickets. During the night, I peeped out, and I saw a sick yellow moon that cast grotesque shadows that clung to the walls of the huts.

That night was the longest ever. The following day was heavy and slow.

Two months after the soldiers displayed the bodies before us, the *vakomana* killed Mbongwe whose four sons working as district assistants. Mbongwe was boastful and would tell anyone who cared to listen that his sons could wipe out all the terrorists. The Rhodesian regime called the *vakomana* terrorists.

Even his sons were notorious for harassing and threatening people when they visited the protected village. And we were so afraid of them because they brought guns with them.

The *vakomana* killed Mbongwe just outside the protected village around 10 in the morning. When the *vakomana* killed Mbongwe, he had gone to his field in Kamoto village.

Between the Kamoto village and the protected village was a veldt. It was around October. The first rains had fallen and the ground was soft. The grass and trees were blooming. The fields had some crops and Bongwe's field was not very far from the protected village. They got him when he was walking back to the protected village - about 120 metres from the western gate. The *vakomana* waited for him in the tall grass that day.

In the early days, a number of the district assistants were from outside the Chiweshe area, but later, local youth were recruited and deployed within their communities. Among these youth were four of Mbongwe's sons.

Mbongwe's killing heightened the fear because it dawned on us that the war was just outside the fence – close by.

The killing also made us realise how the situation had gotten out of hand. We wondered just how vakomana could have waited in the tall grass just outside the gate for Mbongwe and then drove a pickaxe through the top of his head – drove it so hard that the pickaxe came out under his chin.

Of course, the *vakomana* disappeared into thin air after killing Mbongwe. But one woman who claimed to have seen what happened said the vakomana did not want to kill Mbongwe.

However, Mbongwe himself had advanced towards them when they asked him to accompany them into the mountains.

When news of Mbongwe's killing filtered into the protected village, the gates were locked up, and those who had gone out had to rush back since the whole area was swarming with soldiers. Three jet fighters took turns flying past the protected village.

Mbongwe's body lay in the October sun from the mid-morning time when he was killed until the following day. That night was filled with gunfire and dogs whimpering in fear. The district assistants also fired flares into the air all night long.

My brothers and I huddled in a corner where father had said if bullets were to be fired at the hut, they would not penetrate easily.

As I stand here looking over where the protected village used to be, I wonder how father thought that bullets would target our hut specifically.

When Mbongwe's body was brought into the protected village, the people gathered at the western gate. All ages. Not even the soldiers who were swarming everywhere like flies scared the people.

The body was in an open Land Rover. It was not covered, and the pickaxe handle was visible. The pickaxe was still stuck in his skull. There were flies following the Land Rover.

We had heard about this war. It had always been far away. But Mbongwe's death changed our minds. Death was among us. The elders spoke in hushed tones as they walked away from the gate where Mbongwe's body had been brought in.

Mbongwe was buried inside the protected village. We heard that efforts to pull out the pickaxe failed, and Mbongwe was buried with the weapon that had killed him stuck in his skull.

You remember, *Mama*, that we spent more than a week locked up in the protected village.

Indeed, *Mama*, the way people live now has changed. I can see huts and houses everywhere even where we used to herd cattle. There are huts and houses lining up on both sides of the road from here. There are more cars now than before.

A lot has also changed. I have been standing here for about an hour now and all the people passing by did not greet me or acknowledge my presence. The few who did look at me suspiciously.

The truck that drove past me carrying people dressed in the ruling party colours and singing party songs slowed down a few metres down the road. The singing stopped and so did my heart. I heard, mama, that the youth are doing bad things to people whose political affiliation is not known.

Just last week, there were reports about teachers who were forced to drink rat killer because they were campaigning for a new opposition party. Some of the teachers were burnt with acid.

I grew up here, *Mama*, but I am a stranger now. Very few if any remembers me. I doubt that this land even recognises me.

There is another truck, *Mama*, carrying more youths. They are singing and waving small ruling party flags.

Wakatamba nemusangano unoparara, they are singing, mama.
Nyika ino ine vanhu pasi, they are saying.
Wakatengesa wazvichekeresa, they continue.
Zvemadhisinyongoro tazviramba, they swear.

It is an election year. It is another time to kill and be killed. It is another time for families to separate. A time for brothers to fight brothers. Parents to disown their children. Children to walk away from their families. This is what election has come to mean in these parts of the world.

One would have thought with time our people grow to understand that politics is just a game. And that our people are the soccer balls.

There was so much hope, mama, when we came from the protected villages. For a few years, this country seemed to be doing well. There were jobs. Schools were free. Industries were working. Even the skies never disappointed. It rained, mama. It rained all the time. We had wet Christmases and good harvests.

Then we heard about the Willowvale scandal. The ministers were buying cars cheaply and selling them at high prices. Then we heard some minister had committed suicide. Others lost their jobs. And Edgar Tekere left the ruling party to start his own party.

Since then, *Mama*, things have never been the same. The Willowvale scandal was a sluice gate to what this country has become.

Do you remember the farms just before Gweshe village, mama? Those farms where the fields were always green with wheat in winter, maize and cotton in summer? Those farms, *Mama*, are now just barren land. Our people chased out the farmer because he supported a new opposition party. Our people took over the land, which is a good thing since the war was about land. All the years we spent in the protected village was because *vakomana* were fighting for land.

I remember, *Mama*, that the government through the reserve bank distributed fertilizers, seeds and farming equipment to our people. You will not believe, *Mama*, that most of those who received the items sold them before they returned to the farms.

Most of those who grabbed the farms sold the irrigation pipes, electrical cables and anything they could lay their hands on. They fished all the dams dry and set about cutting down the trees on the farms. They then sold the firewood, stacking them by roadside.

Today, those big farms have become small villages where people wait for the rains so that they can plough just a corner of those big fields. The worst part, mama, is that those who grabbed farms use the ruling party as a reason for sitting on land that could produce enough not only for this country but the region. Is that not why this country was called the breadbasket of southern Africa?

We are here, *Mama*, where we now have to buy maize from Zambia where some of the white farmers sought refuge. We are here, mama, where we have to rely on South Africa for groceries, most of which this country used to produce in abundance.

And talking about Zambia and South Africa, *Mama*, do you know that every youth is trying to leave this country? Yes, *Mama*, they are. If you ask these days, you will hear about people going to London, Australia, America, and Canada. In fact, *Mama*, there is a joke that our people are found in Iceland.

They are running away, mama. Running away from independence and elections. They are running away from violence. Running away from poverty. And joblessness.

Yes, *Mama*, they are all running away to find new lives elsewhere. Most of the people in this village left. The old people are living lonely lives now.

But again, *Mama*, some are dying. I have heard that quite a number have died in foreign lands. They died alone. Those who left as husband and wife, separated once they left.

Who ever thought, *Mama*, that this country would become a river that flows blood? Back then, mama, you remember how it rained. You remember how the land gave so much food. You remember how this village was so loving and accommodating.

We used to mock Mozambicans running away from the civil war caused by the Matsanga. They came into the villages looking for jobs and new lives. We mocked them calling them *ma*Moscan.

I am told that our people are crossing into Mozambique today to buy food and second-hand clothes.

What have they done to this country, *Mama*? Why is there so much fear on people's faces? There is hesitation and doubt.

Maybe, *Mama*, you still recall the song we used to sing about a country that became a river of blood? A country that had ceased to be a home? A country that ate its own people? A country where people knew no laughter but sadness, fear and sorrow?

Yes, mama, that song where the singer would then appeal to God to come and rescue the people. This here, *Mama*, is that country.

Imagine that Harare is worse than the remotest village, *Mama*. There is no water and people are drilling boreholes. Drilling boreholes in Harare, *Mama*. The roads are torn and electricity is a luxury.

Everyone is now a business person, selling anything they can lay their hands on. Imagine also, *Mama*, that this country has some of the richest people who do not lose an opportunity to show off their wealth.

The ministers, their families and those close to the power are living as if they are in a different country. Amid all the poverty and deprivation, *Mama*, people are driving the latest million-dollar cars and building mansions.

I stopped to imagine a God up there, mama. Where is He when some of his people are living like orphans in a country that promised them so much but ended up taking away everything?

Don't they say the more things change, the more they remain the same? Yes, *Mama*, just like when the war ended and the youth were sent out to harass, beat and sometime kill for the party, today it is happening.

That too, mama, just like death has not changed. Do you still remember how *babamunini* Charakupa's houses were burnt during the 1980 campaign? We had just returned to the villages from the protected villages then. *Babamunini* Charakupa supported that bishop's party.

I hear the same is happening again here, mama. Village against village. Father against sons. Brothers against brothers. They are beating up each other again. This is what independence mean. We do not see white soldiers coming to close down schools and grinding mills any more. Our brothers and fathers are doing that now.

I hear you cannot get a piece of land here if you do not support the ruling party. Some have had their land taken because they do not support the ruling party. The same happened with the farms.

So much has changed yet so little has changed. Wait, *Mama*, I hear some singing. It is coming from a big tent visible from here. Could be a new church, *Mama*. There are a lot of them here now.

Churches have become sanctuaries in these parts of the country. People go pray for wealth. And almost every enterprising person has become some kind of a prophet. Most of them are youth, *Mama*.

Yes, mama, things do not change. It is the people and time that change. Do you remember when we returned to this village from the protected villages, *Mama*? There were new churches everywhere.

The tent I see from here is the same size like the one that was put up a few weeks after we came back from the protected villages.

Is that not when some girls in this village were left pregnant by the youthful pastors? But yes, the villages were set alight with revivalist gospel. There was a band and a choir. Every evening, we gathered in the tent to dance and marvel at the youthful pastors.

How can I forget one song they used to sing at the opening and the closing of every night's sermon, *Mama*?

It was about power in the blood of Jesus. That power was greater than baba vako, the singers would shout. The power that is greater than amai vako, they added.

But a few months after they moved to Gunguhwe area just beyond those grey hills, *Mama*, the village realised that three girls were pregnant. The pastors never came back.

But I have come back, *Mama*. I am here. I wanted to be here but now I am asking myself why I have come. I wonder if there is anything left for me here.

Memories, yes, *Mama*. A lot of memories. Old wounds, yes. Opening old wounds until they start bleeding.

Can you imagine that all the people who passed by here did not even greet me? They hurried past me the same way people in Harare race past.

Maybe you are wondering why I am back here, mama. Like I said when I alighted the bus, I came to bury myself. Noone wants to die alone, mama. As I grow older, the fear of dying alone engulfs me all the time.

Sometimes I wake up sweating during the night. Then I have this vision of being alone when incapacitation comes. I saw what happened to my brothers when they could not help themselves. Those scenes play in my mind and a deep fear wash over me.

There is no joy in growing old, *Mama*. What joy can be there when one loses parts of oneself each passing day. I do not know about others though, *Mama*, but I know for certain that growing old alone is so scary.

Maybe you are still wondering why I came back, mama. The truth is I am afraid of everything. The beginning scares me. This present scares me. And the end too, scares me.

The truth is I am lonely.

I have accommodated loneliness long enough to be scared of it. I scatter people close to me. Just like all of you died and left me alone. Every single one who dares come close to me leaves. They always find a reason to leave. For some unexplained reason, I let them leave.

I do not ask them to stay. I do not ask them why they are going. Just like I never asked any of you why you were dying. I lived on. I moved on. I hid the pain of the losses. It was like burying treasure. It is only that this treasure always finds me, unlike other treasures that can never be found. Every memory I try to push to the back of my mind finds a place at the front.

This conversation with you, *Mama*, is one such long memory. My mind always regrets being me. I ask myself if it could have turned any different; suppose I was born in another family, by another mother and father.

But I heard we cannot choose our families. At least, that is one thing that will never change. Family will always be family.

That mama is what scares me. Everything about me scares me.

Yes, mama, I am afraid of dying alone. You know, I often visualise a dog's life in its old age. Sickly. Weak. Sores on its skin. Flies everywhere. Wounds on its ears. And unable to fend for itself. Cruel people are kicking it out of their way. Children throwing stones and chasing them down the street.

That kind of thing, *Mama*, because dogs' lives are like that in the end. Mostly. No sister. No brother. And no cousins. Just a dog. When it finally dies, no one buries it. It will lie in the sun. Eaten by flies and scavengers. And its bones scattered when scavengers have eaten all the flesh.

That is my biggest fear, *Mama*. The long nights when sleep refuses to come. When the mind stays awake and travels to places unknown. When the bones carry the pain. And when needles run through the veins.

The mornings become just the start of some different pain. And looking into this future of more pain. Yes, *Mama*, unknown ailments love an old body.

This pain could have been better if the heart was at peace, *Mama*. My heart has never known peace. I mean real love, mama. I have lived a life of empty hearts. It does not help that I have a sharp mind. The heart has the keys to happiness.

Yes, *Mama*, she threw me out of the house. Our house, *Mama*. Just like that. But I could have seen it coming. Even felt it coming. I did not because I used my mind and not my heart.

I do not just wake up one morning and leave or ask the other to go, mama. It is a build-up of heavy silence and sometimes noisy days. Either way, *Mama*, silence, and noise in a relationship have the same effects. You suffer equally the same.

Silence gnaws at you until your heart and mind become empty of emotions. It scares you until you fear going back home. It makes you suspicious of the other's motives and watches their every move.

Noise in a relationship angers and drains you. It takes so much energy and fills your mind with revenge. The words have a way of weakening you and marinating your personality.

Well, *Mama*, we never quarrelled. But the silence weighed us down each day. It got to an extent where I could not fathom going home. I would leave one bar to the next just so the night lengthens and I get home late.

I was not alone, *Mama*. We ended up as a group of men who feared going back home to their wives. We drank all night and moved on to the next one when the bar closed.

Looking back now, I realise that I was not escaping but trapping myself. I do not know about other men, but I know they never escaped from whatever or whoever they were running away from.

As for me, here I am, *Mama*. No partner. No child. No family. Here I am back here to search for family and to wait to join you in the Nyota Hills.

Much of the pain comes from not knowing what went wrong. It comes from not knowing who to blame. It would alleviate the pain if I could blame someone.

But there is no one. Not me. Not her. Whatever happened started silently and advanced stealthily.

The problem, mama, is knowing exactly how it started. I know it started, but I cannot tell how it did.

How I wished to have a family, *Mama*. To grow old in some woman's arms. To see our grandchildren living with us. To die in some woman's arms. To know that when you lie and never rise again, your family will be with you. Someone will always hold your hand and assure you everything is alright, even when they know nothing is okay.

There is comfort in knowing that you share the pain and hopelessness with other people. And when you finally get knocked out, they will hold you dear in their hearts.

The pain, *Mama*, of not knowing how something so good or meant to have been good fell apart is greatest. Knowing what would have gone wrong gives room for solutions. You know the problem; therefore, you should work out a solution.

Well, mama, it is not like we did not try to patch up things. Yes, mama, patch them up because nothing was broken but torn. Since none of us knew what was wrong, we found no solution. Our conversations ended up in circles and created more bottomless voids.

What always came out was that none of us was at fault, yet we knew our marriage was not working. I always had one question, though - it was about us. The two of us. We had issues, yet none took the blame.

It escalated, but I cannot say what exactly escalated.

And here I am, *Mama*.

Mmap Fiction and Drama Series

If you have enjoyed *Conversation With My Mother* consider these other fine books in **Mmap Fiction and Drama Series** from *Mwanaka Media and Publishing:*

The Water Cycle by Andrew Nyongesa
A Conversation…, A Contact by Tendai Rinos Mwanaka
A Dark Energy by Tendai Rinos Mwanaka
Keys in the River: New and Collected Stories by Tendai Rinos Mwanaka
How The Twins Grew Up/Makurire Akaita Mapatya by Milutin Djurickovic and Tendai Rinos Mwanaka
White Man Walking by John Eppel
The Big Noise and Other Noises by Christopher Kudyahakudadirwe
Tiny Human Protection Agency by Megan Landman
Ashes by Ken Weene and Umar O. Abdul
Notes From A Modern Chimurenga: Collected Struggle Stories by Tendai Rinos Mwanaka
Another Chance by Chinweike Ofodile
Pano Chalo/Frown of the Great by Stephen Mpashi, translated by Austin Kaluba
Kumafulatsi by Wonder Guchu
The Policeman Also Dies and Other Plays by Solomon A. Awuzie
Fragmented Lives by Imali J Abala
In the Beyond by Talent Madhuku
Zororo Risina Zororo by Oscar Gwiriri
Sword of Vengeance by Olatubosun David
Finding A Way Home by Tendai Mwanaka

Your Epistle by Solomon A Awuzie
The Restless Run and Ruin of the Roaches and Rats by McLayode
The Reign of Terror by Ntando Gerald
Ibala Lyabwina Nama by Austin Kaluba
Daddy, Please Don't Kill Mama by Natisha Parsons
Pilate's Angels by Goodenough Mashego
Blue threads and other stories by Matthew Kunashe Chikono
The Sylvia Plath Effect by Abigail George
The Twins by Shakemore Dirani
I, Robert's Robot and other stories by Marvel Chukwudi Pephel

Soon to be released

https://facebook.com/MwanakaMediaAndPublishing/

www.ingramcontent.com/pod-product-compliance
Lightning Source LLC
Chambersburg PA
CBHW061524050726
47503CB00016B/2716